MW01519616

FOUND : A BODY

Poetry by Betsy Struthers

Saying So Out Loud. Oakville, Ont.: Mosaic Press, 1988

Censored Letters. Oakville, Ont.: Mosaic Press, 1984

FOUND : A BODY

BETSY STRUTHERS

⊞Simon & Pierre
Toronto, Canada

We would like to express our gratitude to The Canada Council, Ontario Arts Council and Ontario Publishing Centre for their support.

Marian M. Wilson, Publisher

1 2 3 4 5 · 7 6 5 4 3

Canadian Cataloguing in Publication
  Struthers, Betsy
      Found: a body.

ISBN 0-88924-237-2

I. Title.

PS8587.T78F6 1992   C813'.54   C92-095168-6
PR9199.3.S87F6 1992

Cover design and illustration: Suzanne Gauthier
Editor: Marian M. Wilson

Printed and bound in Canada.

Order from:
Simon & Pierre Publishing Co. Ltd./
Les Editions Simon & Pierre Ltée
P.O. Box 280, Adelaide St. Postal Stn.
Toronto, Ontario, Canada M5C 2J4

for my grandmother, Pauline Day,
who introduced me to the
literary art of murder

Acknowledgements

I thank the Canada Council whose grant funding another literary project gave me time in which I also wrote this book. For their advice and encouragement, I thank Cary Gillespie, Rob Gillespie, Don LePan, Steven O'Connor, Angela Rebeiro, Leonie Van Ness, and Eric Wright; and especially, Ned Struthers; and always, Jim Struthers.

ONE

"Sadie," I called, "where are you? Come here."

Gulls erupted from a thicket of alders along the river bank. They shrieked as they wheeled in tight loops low over the water and back above the shore. My dog yelped in short, excited bursts, her voice the squeal of chalk on a wet blackboard.

"Sadie."

She came, reluctantly, whining now, her head turned back towards her find. I took hold of the collar, a red leather loop half hidden in her thick black ruff. She stood waist high, her size and long nose inherited from her Shepherd mother, her colour and gentle nature from the father I assumed was a Labrador retriever. We often walked in the park together, even here in the bush which grew wild along the river bank on the shore opposite to town. I'd read stories of violence committed here, an occasional rape, muggings, beatings. But I never worried when Sadie paced at my heel, her head swinging between her shoulders, tongue lolling between pointed teeth. No one ever dared to bother the two of us.

I thought this time she might have found a wounded duck or dead fish. Thankful that I was wearing boots, I waded into the river to circle the bushes which threw their tangle of branches low over the shoreline. She broke away from me and bounded off in great splashing leaps. I wiped off my glasses with the cuff of one sleeve.

"Sadie, Sadie."

My voice echoed. How quiet it was at three o'clock in the

afternoon, children still in school, the park deserted. I could see only one other person in all that distance, a woman in a brown coat and scarf who shrank as she hurried across the long footbridge towards downtown. Even if she stopped to look for a moment at the ducks who waited beneath the bridge for the scraps of bread that mothers taught their toddlers to throw, she wouldn't hear my voice against the grumble of water over the hydro dam. She wouldn't even see me, hidden as I was by the willow trees, the fall of land. A small wind rattled the few leaves remaining on the trees and rippled the river in waves that lapped against my feet. Through the rubber boots, it was icy cold.

Sadie began to bark hysterically. I pushed through the outer bushes and almost fell. Legs bare as peeled sticks blocked my path, spiked red heels bobbing on the current. I stepped back, grabbed a willow branch as my knees buckled. Water sloshed into my right boot, soaked my pant leg, my sock. Eyes closed, I shook my head, but when I opened them she was still there, more terrible and real than any vision.

It was a woman, naked except for those fancy shoes, their dye bleeding into the water. She was face down, the rise and fall of waves lifting and dropping her torso in a parody of breath, her arms outflung, the fingers curled as if grasping at the trailing roots that snagged her. Her hair was long and lay like stranded weeds in black strips across her shoulders and drifted, an uneven halo, around her head. Wounds the size of quarters dotted her back. There was no blood but purple bruises and deep scratches scored her skin where she had tumbled and scraped against the rocks of the whirlpool farther upstream below the dam. A crow shrieked from the top of a willow and the gulls took up the cry. I had disturbed their feast.

Sadie was back with me now, pushing her head against my thighs, nosing me closer. I grabbed her collar again, attached the leash, backed away. More water slopped into my boots. I was out too deep, but didn't care. Sadie growled and tried to pull away;

we both stumbled through mud to shore where I knelt, shivering. She licked my face. Three more gulls flew in towards the trees, provoking a loud cacophony of greed.

I wanted to run as fast and far away as I could. What held me back was the time. School was out and soon children would be coming home across the bridge; as always, a gang of the more adventurous would detour down the river trail to play in the woods and reeds. What if one of them should stumble over that thing back there? I would spare them that horror. The nearest house was still a football field away across the park. I wouldn't be able to get there, talk my way into using the telephone, and get back in time to stop them.

Where were my neighbours? The screaming of the birds made me sick. I threw up, bile burning my stomach, my throat, my lips. Looking up at last, I saw two small girls staring at me from the safety of the footbridge.

"Please," I called out to them, "I need some help." I waved my arms, beckoning them to come closer, to listen to me.

They giggled and ran, thinking, I'm sure, that I was drunk, one of the homeless who sometimes wandered this far from the town centre, looking for solitude, for peace. Perhaps they were only afraid of Sadie who panted in my grasp, drool dangling from her open jaws. My hair was in a tangle, glasses crooked and smudged with tears, vomit stains on my sweater, mud on my jeans. I probably looked like the kind of stranger they were taught to fear.

Another dog rescued us. I recognized its mistress, Ada Wilcox, a widow who lived down the street from me. As usual she wore a long black coat and a head scarf which, though knotted tightly, could not contain her wiry white curls. Her ankles, wrapped in thick support hose, trembled above sturdy black shoes. Once I had overheard some children on the street call her home the "witch's house"; blinds always drawn and grass left lank and weed-ridden, it deserved its name. She poked her cane into the soft earth and yanked her poodle's long lead.

I jumped up, steadying myself against Sadie. Ada stepped back, raising her stick.

"What do you want?" she snapped.

"Help."

She peered at me, her nose wrinkling as a whiff of the stains on my sweater and jeans reached her. Then she nodded. "I know you. You live in the corner house, right? Robinson's place, that was."

"That's right. I'm Rosalie Cairns." I stuck my hand out in greeting, but let it drop when she ignored it. My glasses slipped again. I pushed them back and brushed away the strands of wet hair from my mouth and eyes.

"Looks like you been in the water," she said. Her lips twitched.

"I found . . ." I stopped and swallowed, began again. "I found a body in the reeds, just down there. A woman, drowned."

She turned to look where I pointed at the alderbushes weeping over the river. "Dead?" she asked.

I nodded.

She looked at me, at the river, at the line of school children now straggling across the bridge. Her dog continued to whine and jump about, almost strangling itself in its eagerness to get closer to Sadie.

"It would be terrible for the kids to see it — her. Will you stay and warn them off while I go for help?"

"A little late for that, isn't it? You found her, you better stay here by her. Who is she?"

"I don't know."

"Well." Ada pursed her lips and glared at the river. "People these days," she muttered and then continued in a louder voice, "I'll send someone along as soon as I can. Come now, Cookie, be a good girl."

She limped off, dragging the poodle behind her. The dog

kept turning back to bark, but finally both disappeared between the stone pillars of the park entrance.

I sank down into the faint warmth of the nest my body had made in the dry grass, my face half-buried in Sadie's hair, my ear full of the even thud of her heart. Although it was such a beautiful day, not one child lingered, perhaps seeing my presence there as an unwelcome challenge.

I don't know how long it took for the police to arrive but they finally came, two patrol cars with sirens blaring and lights flashing. They had to leave the cars by the park gates which were chained open only wide enough for a person to slip through. I almost laughed to see them run across the field, four large men clumsy with overladen belts, one already holding a portable radio to his mouth.

After that came the questions from the detectives who waited with me while the corpse was landed, and from the reporters who flashed pictures of everything in sight, the ducks, the dog, the body bundled in black plastic on a wheeled stretcher that bumped over the hummocks of the field, tossing its burden from side to side while a white-coated attendant steadied it, his hands pink and raw. A small crowd pressed against the sawhorse barriers the patrolmen placed around the park gate. Some neighbours recognized me as I hurried to my house on the next corner. That night the phone rang and rang until Will, my husband, knocked the headset from its cradle and left it buzzing on the counter between a pizza box and an empty case of beer.

Even in a small town, suicide quickly becomes yesterday's story. Who was she and why had she chosen our river in which to end her life? The local news worried over the mystery for less than a week. Then the headlines turned to reports of a paving contract scandal and kickbacks to local politicians.

My best friend, Karen Lewis, brought the Toronto newspapers over on Saturday morning. She lived right downtown, but often rode her ten-speed across the footbridge to visit us. Along with the papers, she had a white paper bag of cinnamon crullers from the donut shop where she always ate breakfast.

"They've found out who she was," she announced, waving the thick roll of newsprint. "She's that Toronto lawyer who's been missing for nearly two weeks. Jennifer Rumble. A hiker found her car in the bush upriver from the dam on one of those deserted railway spurlines. She'd left all her clothes neatly folded on the front seat on top of her purse and keys."

"Except her shoes," I said. I shivered at the memory of those red spikes. They haunted my dreams.

"Jennifer Rumble," Will repeated. "I met her once, years ago, when I was still with the Immigration Department. She handled the appeal for a Salvadorean family. We suspected the guy was connected to one of the cartels, but she claimed political persecution if he went back. There were a couple of kids too and the wife was pregnant. They stayed." He brooded over the newspaper publicity shot that advertised her partnership in a Toronto firm. "She was beautiful, talented. It's hard to believe." He shook his head, dropped the paper. "Who wants more coffee?"

"What was she like?" I asked, reaching for the paper. I also stared at the picture, trying to attach that face to the body I had found.

"You know lawyers," Will called from the kitchen. "Nice enough until she got what she wanted. I didn't see much of her after that case was settled." The refrigerator door sighed and thudded, milk poured, a sugar spoon clicked around a mug.

"I wonder what she was doing here?" I said.

Karen scanned the story. "She was born here, but her family moved away when she was little. She wasn't married, had no kids of her own. Maybe she still thought of this as a place to come home to, to die in."

"What a lonely way to die." The weather had turned. Fog obscured the view of the river.

Will ambled back into the living room. Although it was early and a Saturday morning, he was dressed for work in a paint-spattered sweatshirt and denims gone white in the knees. He placed the steaming cup carefully on a stack of paperbacks that occupied the top of the pine blanket box we used for a coffee table. "For you," he said. His left hand brushed back over his head, the gold of his ring gleaming through thick chestnut hair graying at the temples. His other hand hovered, then gripped my shoulder. "You'll be all right?"

My cheek caressed the fine hairs of his wrist. "I'm fine. Really. Will you be coming home for lunch?"

"I doubt it."

"Aren't you on shift today?" Karen interrupted. She and I both worked part-time in the same bookstore; in fact, I got her the job there when she moved back to town a year ago, after her father died. He had always hoped she would follow him into the family business, a pharmacy founded by his grandfather. She had no intention of doing so: she hated the smell of the drug counter and the questions of the customers. Her parents finally agreed to support her way through teacher's college, expecting that she would apply for a position in the local high school and live at home until she married. Instead, she took off the day after graduation with a boy she met at a rock concert. Her father never forgave her.

She lived in California for awhile, working in a health food co-op, then thumbed her way around Europe and Africa. After a stint in an Israeli kibbutz, she moved to Vancouver where she supported herself in a variety of odd jobs, chiefly in the social service sector. She'd had various lovers, but none had lasted long. "I'm irredeemably single," she always said.

Now she was juggling the part-time job in the bookstore with classes at teacher's college to update her training. Like Will and me, she was almost forty and beginning to fear old age, the pension years. She had the patience and creativity to be a good teacher, though it was hard to imagine her in a structured setting. I was very glad to have her living close by. With Will so busy setting up his business, it was a relief to me to have such a good friend to talk to.

"I've got the morning," I answered her, "and Stephanie's on this afternoon. If she pulls her usual Saturday stunt, I'll be there all day. She always has some excuse to avoid working weekends."

"I'll call you about noon then," Will decided. "What are we going to do about dinner? Do you want to take something out of the freezer before you go?"

"Let's go out instead, somewhere interesting."

"In this town?" Karen snorted. She rooted through the sections of newspaper for her bag, a black canvas backpack stuffed with papers, tissues, a spiral bound notebook, a handful of pens. She stood, draping it over her shoulder, one buckle catching for a moment in the loose weave of her apple-green sweater. Patting her jeans pockets, she smiled slightly at the bulge of keys against her fingers. Finally, she picked up a black beret from a bowl of apples on the table and angled it over one eye, tucking in every wisp of red hair.

"I've got to run. I promised Mom I'd go to the market with her this morning, after I saw you. She's still nagging me about giving up my place and moving in with her. I know she's lonely, but I keep telling her I've got my own life. What life? she asks. A bachelor apartment and a part-time job. I'm going to college, I say. You're too old for college, she says. You should be teaching already. If you hadn't wasted all those years, moving from one end of the globe to the other, from job to job, you might have a husband, children, a proper home." She rolled her eyes, her shoulders exaggerating a shrug. "I can't win, but at least I won't have to feel guilty —" she paused, "today."

We all laughed.

Will checked his watch. "I've got to go, too."

"What are you working on today?" I asked.

He grimaced. "The Martins again. She still hasn't made up her mind about the countertops for the kitchen. I can't do anything more until that's settled. I've got some more samples to take over there. And then I've got an estimate on a bathroom out on the fourth line. Jerry'll need the truck, so I'll have to take the car. Do you need it?"

I shook my head. "What time will you be home?"

He shrugged, pulling on the blue leather windbreaker he'd been wearing since college, the gold letters faded now to a dull brown, the elbows bleached and webbed with fine cracks. Three of the snaps had fallen out, leaving neat holes down the left front. He didn't bother trying to close it anyway. Although he still carried himself like the basketball forward he'd been, light and easy on his feet, his body was beginning to thicken and settle.

Will was in better shape now than he'd been during the years he worked in government. He'd started as a clerk in the Immigration Department in a summer job wangled through an uncle; then he worked his way up the bureaucratic ladder moving from Ottawa to Toronto, from minor case loads to major crises as the refugee situation worsened. He finally quit four years ago. His mother blamed his move on trendiness, the penchant for male mid-life change. But he'd seen three of his colleagues die of heart attacks before they turned fifty, others juggling two families, dealing with bitter ex-wives and rebellious children.

He had always wanted to work with his hands, to turn his love for carpentry into a full-time profession. The building boom had made it possible for him to realize his dream. We moved from Toronto northeast to Karen's hometown, where cheaper house prices were encouraging young professional couples to settle down and renovate. The fact that he was working longer hours, including weekends, while earning less money than ever, didn't seem to bother him. I was getting used to suppers alone, long evenings with only Sadie for company.

They left together. Karen flew on her bike down the hill to the park, one hand raised in farewell. Will backed the Honda out of the garage, easing between the huge maples that flanked the driveway. Red leaves spun and drifted in his wake. Sadie pressed her wet nose into my hand. "Work today," I told her. I closed the front door and led her through the kitchen where I slid open the patio door. As she bounced down the step, I grabbed a bone from the fridge and threw it out to her. She caught it in mid-air.

TWO

It was the first time I'd walked through the park since finding Jennifer Rumble's body a week ago. I glanced down the hill to the river bank where a few stray ribbons of yellow plastic still marked the site. I stayed on the tarred path that led from my street to the footbridge. Built of wooden boards suspended on steel struts, it stretched between stone pylons in a gentle curve towards the other shore, almost two hundred yards distant. A couple of teenagers on bicycles called a warning as they raced for the gates. Two joggers pounded by on either side of me. High heels clicked impatiently behind me, and I moved aside to let a woman pass. She nodded, barely pausing as she hurried across to her job in a store or office that demanded a dress code of skirt and stockings. I wore my usual working clothes, a blouse and cardigan, cord pants and walking shoes, a tote bag heavy with paperbacks, a coffee thermos, an apple. I slowed as I crossed the bridge. I liked to look at the river and count the ducks, even on mornings like this when fog wreathed the river banks, and the water growled as it rushed unseen over the dam.

A man leaned on the railing close to the far shore. He glanced my way, then turned his head abruptly, one hand half covering his face. I looked around. The park was now empty.

Keep going, I told myself, just ignore him. He's not interested in you.

A crow cawed and I opened my eyes wide against the sudden vision of pale flesh pitted with red wounds.

She did it to herself. I chanted the phrase like a mantra, a spell against the visions which still woke me every night.

All the same, as if I might be called upon to provide a statement, I took careful note of his appearance: red toque pulled low over thick brown hair; moustache, no beard; red plaid jacket, blue jeans, running shoes; a black and red sports bag at his feet. I held my own bag tighter, keys bristling in my fist. I wished Sadie was with me. But when I passed behind him, he didn't look up from his study of the current's swirl. I stepped off the bridge and looked back. He had straightened and was staring my way, straight at me. As I watched, he bent to pick up his bag.

I turned and hurried along residential streets, the houses leaning together the closer I got to downtown. Motorcycles were parked on several of the bare dirt lawns; porches sagged beneath the weight of abandoned sofas, boxes, and cats. It was early and cold; no one was outdoors. I imagined parents lying late in bed, children planted in front of television sets. Cars lined both sides of the streets, the branches of old maples hanging low over their hoods. Some leaves had caught in the filigree of hedges but most had been swept away, the earth indecent in these last days before the snow.

I stopped for a moment in front of the police station, debating whether to go in, risking another glance behind. The street was empty.

You idiot, I said to myself, he was just some guy on his way to the Y for a squash game, a swim. Nothing to do with you. Stop being so paranoid.

The fountain of the courthouse lawn was clogged with paper bags and more leaves, a filthy puddle shivering in the slight cold wind. I walked faster to rid myself of the chill that trembled my lips, my fists thrust deep in my pockets. I crossed streets with traffic lights, where the buildings were all three storey and commercial: a pizza parlour, a beauty salon, a new-to-you clothing exchange, a discount store. There were more cars on the road here, signal lights blinking as drivers searched for a free meter, buses snorting as they waited for their passengers to get off or on.

Three blocks away, the clock tower loomed over the town centre, its hands as usual set wrong, too slow or too fast, I couldn't tell. Soon the businessmen's association would program it with tapes of carols to play every half hour, treacly organ and chime versions of "O Come All Ye Faithful" to entice shoppers into stores whose windows were already crammed with gifts. Green tinsel banners stretched across the hydro lines between the taller buildings and wreaths and candles decorated every second pole.

On Saturdays, two teen-agers dressed as elves would give candy canes to all the children out shopping with their parents. I would start finding cellophane wrappers and discarded suckers stuck to the picture books on the bottom shelves. People would complain loudly and expensive art books would disappear, hidden under down parkas and in parcels bulging with legitimate purchases, sweaters and socks.

The Pocket Book was a small store, jammed between a dress shop for ladies of a certain age and a gift shop whose window featured families of ceramic mice, silk flowers in coloured glass bowls, teddy bears dressed up in seasonally appropriate knitted garments. The gift shop's owner was a thin, sharp-featured woman whose long black hair trailed over shoulders clad always in sweaters of uncertain colour and manufacture. She came in once every two weeks to buy six romance novels, all newly published but often by the same author and always with the same *Wuthering Heights* cover art. She never talked.

Unlike most of our regular customers. The one I called the Pink Lady was already at the door, peering through thick glasses at the window exhibit of novels and histories of war commemorating Remembrance Day. It was my job to change it that morning. I'd been planning all weekend to put in books on coping with winter, travel guides and Dickens.

Miss Simpson wore an ordinary brown coat and leather boots, but her knitted hat, scarf and gloves were a bright magenta. She varied the shade with the season: in spring, pastel pink; for summer, ice cream colours or florid cherry; in fall, the violent tones; in winter, scarlets and deep rose: to counteract the cold, she said. Her lipstick and nail polish always matched. She never married, but had taken care of her parents until they died. Now, she lived alone in their spacious home in the professional enclave in the old west part of town. "It's so nice," she often said, "that since you must work, you were able to find a job that is so congenial."

The Pink Lady clutched her oversize bag under her arm and squinted through the glass into the darkened interior as if she expected that I was in there, hiding. We never agreed on titles, but she did buy books by the armful, destined for nieces and nephews I hadn't met, so could only imagine their faces on birthday mornings when they opened another package from their aunt: books of romantic history, classic literature, illustrated biographies of European royalty. I knew she read them all first, because she returned unsuitable ones, pages still crisp, but with the covers suspiciously creased. I never argued, but let her take anything in exchange, anything to get her out of the store. She liked to discuss what she'd been reading, mixing up the story lines, confusing characters, distorting history. She pried into my life by telling me intimate stories about her brothers and their families as if I cared, as if I might answer with some gossip of my own.

"You're late this morning," she said. "I've been here five minutes already. I should think you'd be interested in encouraging custom. It's not," she sniffed as I reached around her with the keys, poking at the lock, "as if you do get a lot of business. And it's so cold, just standing here."

She pushed in past me, before I had a chance to turn on the lights. The fluorescent glow at the back of the store illuminated the lurid posters that one of my co-workers had put up for

Hallowe'en. Since no one else wanted to bother with them, I guessed I had better start my day by taking them down.

I was one of four women who worked part-time shifts in the store. The owner, Dr. Long, was a gynecologist who lived in Toronto. She came in to town once a month to pick up the receipts to take to her accountant in the city and to make sure the place was clean and that one of us was on duty. The store was a tax write-off for her. She bought the business along with the property as a retirement investment, then discovered that she could make money by keeping the store going with minimal effort on her part.

The two busy seasons — summer tourists and Christmas shoppers — were bracketed by long days when sometimes only a single customer walked in, and then only to browse, not buy. The previous owner had negotiated a contract with the local separate school board to provide textbooks and stock for its libraries; public school librarians from three surrounding counties came in regularly as well, to buy new books in bulk. We also did special orders for the faculty at the local university and community college. Finding the books they wanted — hardcover academic treatises usually published by American universities — involved a lot of paperwork, but the mark-up made the service pay. Because we did find the books and got them in fairly quickly, these orders kept coming. The store's operating costs were covered by the schools and the academics. Like most retail jobs in town, our salaries were minimum wage and without benefits. However, it was a pleasant job — we chose to sell what we wanted to read and could refer all complaints to a box number in the city. Books were there, and the customers few and far between.

Miss Simpson had her purchases ready: the last Danielle Steele sandwiched between a picture book of the latest royal wedding and the Times crossword paperback. Did she think I wouldn't notice the romance? She chattered while I computed the total on the ancient adding machine that squatted beside the cash register.

"I haven't seen you all week," she said, but didn't wait for me to answer. This was just as well, since I didn't plan on giving her any excuse to stay and talk. She never needed encouragement, was happy to take silence for interest. "I was telling the other girls, Diane is coming to visit for a few weeks. I'm so excited. She's my favourite niece, my brother Geoffrey's girl. She and her husband are going to stay at the cottage. On Mud Lake, not far away at all. I was hoping they'd live with me, I just rattle around in that big house, but you know how young people must have their privacy. It will be so lovely to have her close for a change. She's always off travelling, so very busy. She says they need a place to relax, somewhere she'll feel at home. When she was a little girl, she used to visit me all the time, but then Geoffrey moved to Toronto and I haven't seen much of her since. I'm rather hoping that she has another reason for wanting to slow down." She simpered. "They've been married five years now. I think she might have some big news to tell me. Now you, you're not the one with children, are you?"

"No," I said and rang up the bill. "That's $36.95."

"You shouldn't wait too long, you know," she continued. "My other brother's girl is having a terrible time of it. Of course she already has two lovely little boys but she has her heart set on a daughter. The younger boy's turning eight soon. Lenore, that's her mother, told me that they've been going to one of those clinics. It doesn't seem right to me. All that fooling around with nature. I mean if it's not meant to be, then there must be a reason, don't you agree?"

"It depends," I said. "Shall I put your books in a bag?"

"Of course. Silly me to keep talking away like this." She counted out pennies and nickels, the correct number of bills. "I know first thing in the morning you're probably short of change."

I hadn't had a chance to take off my coat, much less count what Lil left in the till last night. We're supposed to go to the bank at the end of each day, leaving only a token amount of cash hidden in a Crown Royal bag behind some envelopes under the desk.

But Lil always left in a great rush, anxious to get home to her husband who resented her job and who would never make dinner for himself. He was close to retirement and grudged the small independence that working allowed his wife. He wanted dinner on the table at six o'clock as always, and no excuse sufficed.

Why Lil put up with him and had put up with his selfishness through thirty-five years of married life, I failed to understand. "You'll see some day," she'd said.

"I wouldn't stand for it," I retorted.

She smiled. "How long have you been married?"

"Almost fifteen years."

"So you're still on your honeymoon."

We both laughed.

Lil pressed on, "You must have been awfully young to get married."

"I was twenty-four. My mother thought I was plenty old enough," I replied.

"To have a family?"

I turned away from that question and began to fiddle with an order form, a pen.

After waiting a moment, Lil asked, "Don't you ever want to have kids?"

"It's not a question of wanting." I answered.

She had the grace to blush.

The bag was where it should be with all yesterday's take intact: $53.65. I'd been here less than five minutes and already had more than half that — which might well be my only sale all morning.

Miss Simpson began talking again about her niece's visit, but I stopped listening. I slipped her books into a plain brown bag, folded the top edge and sealed it with tape.

Dr. Long didn't believe in spending money on advertising

gimmicks like bookmarks or printed shopping bags. "Useless," she snorted when Karen suggested it to her at one of our rare shop meetings. "They just get thrown out with the rest of the trash." Later, we agreed she was referring to the books as well. None of us had ever seen her pick one up, nor could we imagine her reading for simple pleasure. Still, our cheques always came on time.

"Call me a cab, will you dear?" Miss Simpson asked. She peered out the window. "Never mind, I think I will walk. I'm meeting my dear girl at that charming little teahouse on River Street. I think she'll find it just as good as any of those places she goes to in the city. Have you been there? Well, if I'm going to walk, I'd better get going. Bye-bye."

The bell above the door tinkled. I didn't bother looking up. A draft riffled the pages of a catalogue that had been left open on the desk, a new mystery circled for my attention. That was my specialty in the shop: ordering and arranging the suspense section. We sold very few hardcovers and the paperback houses pushed books that ranged from genteel country house murders to sado-masochistic sleaze. Catalogue blurbs told one story, book reviews another. *The Bare Secret* by Shane Forrest. I could forget that one.

A mittened hand slammed a slim red-covered volume on the desk. "How long, Oh Lord, will this filth be sold here?" roared a too familiar voice.

Ian Dunstable was another regular, a man we called the Reverend. A lay preacher in a revivalist sect, he came into the store every six weeks or so to check if we had stock of *The Catcher in the Rye*, *The Diviners*, and whatever other books his pentecostal assembly decided to censor. He was tall, thin, his narrow face a map of prominent veins and deep angular wrinkles, his fingers twisted by anger or arthritis into yellowed claws. His gray trenchcoat swung open to reveal the shiny blue pin-stripe suit he habitually wore. His left hand tugged at his necktie, his long neck stretching away from the knot, his adam's apple bobbing.

He spoke with a fine spray of spit. I backed away.

"Filth and degeneracy," he shouted. "Where are the good books? The Good Book itself? Where are the decent, moral stories that will teach our children right from wrong? This," he said, shaking the book as if to rattle out its words like sand from gravel, "this is an abomination."

"It's just a book," I answered, not wanting to provoke him further. It was useless. I had to listen to fifteen minutes of rant before he ran out of steam.

Luckily, I had Dr. Long's absence to rely on. "You can complain to the owner," I said. "She'll be so interested to hear your views." I wrote the box number and postal code on a piece of paper and handed it over.

The Reverend stared at it as if it might start to smoke and turn to fire in his hand. "I've written before," he said. He glanced at the one other customer who was looking at the spines of bestsellers in the rack to the right of the door.

I wondered if Dr. Long ever checked that post office box. She had a phone number, too, but it was unlisted, and we dared not use it except in case of real emergency, fire or major theft. Anything else, especially something like this, would cost us our jobs.

Dunstable was still standing there, staring at me.

"May I help you?" I asked.

"Perhaps," he replied. He leaned closer. His breath was a ripe mixture of mint and bacon as he thrust his face forward, his hands tense on the counter.

"Excuse me. I have a customer," I said, nodding towards the man by the door. He didn't turn around. He was listening to the Reverend, I bet, enjoying this scene as only an audience could. As I would, later, enjoy telling Lil and Karen, even Stephanie.

The Reverend ignored him. "Have you taken Jesus into your heart?" he demanded. "Will you pray with me now?"

He lowered his head and, closing his eyes, began to pray out loud. He tried to grab my hand, but I retreated back behind the cash register, arms folded across my chest. I could see that he was working himself up again, that I might be in for one of those sermons that made his chapel renowned among the reborn.

On the floor, a stack of books, unpacked but not sorted or shelved, leaned against the desk. I stretched out one foot and gave a good hard nudge. The books tumbled with a satisfying crash. Dunstable stopped dead in mid-sentence, his eyes wide.

"Oh no," I moaned, "It'll take hours to get these all organized again." I got down on my knees and began to arrange the books in neat piles.

Dunstable waited for a few minutes, but recognized defeat. "God be with you," he grunted, and left.

What a relief. I sat back on my heels and looked at the title in my hand. It was an anthology of short stories about mothers and daughters. I began to thumb through the pages, pausing at paragraphs here and there until I became aware that the other man was staring at me. A tall, brown-haired man, hand over his smile, his moustache. Red plaid shirt jacket and blue jeans. Red and black tote bag over one shoulder. The man on the bridge.

THREE

"I know you." He stated it simply, without a question.

I looked him over carefully, thinking he might be one of Will's clients or a teacher at Karen's school.

"From way back," he said, smiling more broadly now.

I tried to picture him without the moustache, with longer hair. "Sorry. I'm not very good at remembering people. I remember names, but not faces."

"Simon Harper," he said. "Remember me?"

"It's been a long time." I cursed myself for using such a cliché. My nails dug into the smooth paper cover of the book, so deeply they left crescent marks across the smiling face of the author. Oh yes, I recognized him now. The moustache was fuller, the hair thinner, the face lined under the even tan. I remembered the firm yielding of those full lips framed by hair that tickled when we kissed. As we did kiss, once.

"It's been too long." He reached over and snared a lock of my bangs. I like to think my hair looks Rosetti-like but it probably appears unkempt. He let the strand slip through his fingers, tugging ever so gently. It fell against my cheek. His hand rested for a moment on my head, then pulled back to stroke his chin. "I couldn't believe it when Annie told me you were living here now. She sends her greetings."

"How is she? We write at Christmas, but I haven't seen her in ages. Is she still living up north? Last time she wrote, she said they were thinking of moving." Here I was, babbling on like a schoolgirl, the girl I was twenty years ago.

He kept up the chat. "They're near Kapuskasing now, still heading north. She seems to love it up there. I couldn't stand the cold myself. They have snow from Thanksgiving till Easter. But she's quite happy, she and Drew. I've got three little second cousins now, you know."

"She sends pictures."

"We had some good times back then." He leaned on the counter. "You used to come to all the dances when my band played. Remember that group I had, 'Simon Says'?"

"Do you still play?"

"God, no. Not seriously, anyway. I own a travel company, YAK Tours. Maybe you've heard about it?"

I shook my head.

"Adventure tours for the bored and wealthy. It stood for Youths, Adults and Kids, but we dropped the youths and kids. Too much trouble. And the tours are challenging stuff: mountain biking in Nepal, trekking through rainforests. We go all around the world."

"That must be fun."

"Oh, it is. I did a lot of travelling myself for awhile, back in the seventies and eighties when everyone else was making their dough. I thought I might as well get something useful out of the experience."

"I thought you were going to be the next Paul Butterfield."

"Dreams don't pay the rent. Or buy the toys." He pointed out the window. "That's my car out there, the Triumph. Have you ever seen such a beauty?"

I turned and peered out the window at a low-slung red car parked at the curb. Even in this morning's dull light, the paint gleamed. A long aerial swayed back and forth in the wind as if dancing already to the hum of speed. "Very nice," I said.

"And you?" He looked around the store. "You own this place?"

I laughed at that. "No, just work here. Part time."

"You've got kids?"

I shook my head.

He continued, "You're a woman of leisure, then."

"Not by choice. There's not a lot of work in a small town these days. And the hours here beat waitressing." I shifted, easing back on my heels. The small talk soothed. We could be any old friends, meeting after a long parting.

"So how come you're living in this burg? I always pictured you as a big city girl."

"It's a long story."

He shrugged, gesturing at the empty store.

"You really want all the details?"

"Of course I do." He smiled, that smile that made my heart turn over. I used to stare for hours at his graduation photo in my grade eleven yearbook. First love is the love that hurts the most and lasts the longest.

"Well, okay. After school, I went to college and got an M.A. in literature."

"Of course," he interjected. "You always had your head in a book."

"I was thinking of going on for a doctorate, but the pressure got to me, the politicking over grants and all the academic games. I lucked into a job in the reference department at the old Metro Library."

"I can't see you as a librarian," he interrupted again. "Too dusty, too dry."

I shrugged. "It wasn't very interesting, but it paid the rent. Then my mother got cancer. I quit my job to be with her."

"I'm sorry to hear that," he said.

"Before she died, I married the fellow I'd been seeing for a long time. It made her happy. We were going to get married anyway, but her illness just brought the date up a bit."

"And you're still married?"

"To the same guy. His name's Will Cairns. You'd like him."

"What's he do? He the one who owns the store?"

"No. He's in business for himself. Renovations and such. That's why we moved here, for his work. He's a terrific carpenter."

"A hands on kind of guy?" Simon's tone made the simple phrase suggestive.

"He's a good man. I love him very much."

"So how long have you been married?"

"Fifteen years."

He whistled. "And no children?"

"Things don't always work out as planned."

"I'm sorry."

I picked at a thread fraying from my shirt cuff. It was time to buy some new clothes. I hated shopping.

"So you like clerking?" Simon changed the subject.

"It's all right. I can read a lot of books and the people are usually interesting. They're not all like the Reverend. He's in a class by himself."

"I'll say."

"What about you? Have you got a family?"

"I have a wife, a house in the city and a time-share in the Islands, two cars and my own plane. No time for kids."

"You married Sharon after all?"

"Who?"

"Sharon. The girl you brought up to Annie's parents' cottage that weekend."

"You remember her?"

My face burned. I still hated her, that blonde girl in the black miniskirt who came with Simon to crash the party Annie arranged for our high school graduation. There were six of us at her cottage for the Victoria Day weekend, not exactly couples but boys and girls together without chaperones. Annie was furious when her cousin Simon arrived with Sharon in tow. But they had also brought a spaghetti dinner which was better than the food we'd been eating out of cans and boxes. He played his guitar and provided the wine we were all too young to buy for ourselves. Later, there was marijuana, an initiation for the six of us. Later still, Simon and I went for a walk on the beach under a full moon. We kissed. It might have gone further except for Sharon. She tried to kill herself with a kitchen knife. Because Simon was out with me. I still dreamed about his hand on my bare breast, the thrust of his groin against my jeans. Annie came screaming down through the dunes, looking for him. He raced back up to the house, put Sharon in his car, and drove off. I hadn't seen him since.

"I haven't thought about Sharon in years." He paused, stroking his beard. "We broke up when the group did. She married Darryl, the bass player. He's an orthodontist now, out in Mississauga or some place like that."

"And your wife?"

"She's a local girl."

"Is that why you're in town?"

He smiled, his eyes lazily looking me up and down. I didn't stand up for his scrutiny, but stayed crouched by the toppled books, itching to do up one more button at the neck of my shirt, not daring to move my hands.

"Do I need an excuse to look up an old friend?" he asked.

"I wouldn't call us exactly friends," I retorted.

"Then what would you call us? Exactly?"

The jingle of the door opening freed me from the need to answer him.

"Simon? Simon! There you are. We've been looking all over for you." Miss Simpson pushed into the store, pulling a woman in after her. I jumped up, dropping the book. The other woman stared at me, her lips set. She was my age but perfectly groomed, her hair swept into careful curls, her face made up so well you could almost believe her complexion was natural. She wore a full length fox fur coat, open to reveal a creamy silk blouse and blue leather skirt.

"I see you've met," the Pink Lady rushed on. "Diane, this is Rosalie Cairns, one of the dear girls who works here, who's always so helpful and good to me. And this, Rosalie, is my niece, Diane, Simon's wife."

Diane held out her hand to me, and smiled, a smile that transformed her face. Perhaps I had only imagined hostility there.

"We should have realized Simon would be here," she drawled. "He always finds the most interesting places. What a funny little store."

Her nails were sharp and she held my hand too long. I could feel her taking an inventory of my person, the long carelessly brushed hair, wire framed glasses, scrubbed face. My flannel shirt was limp and faded from too many washings, my gray cords bagged at the knees.

"We're old friends," Simon said. "We knew each other ages ago. Rosie was my cousin Annie's best friend in high school."

"You knew another friend of ours, I believe." Diane tucked her arm into Simon's. Her aunt simpered at the picture perfect couple that they made, tall and slim and handsome.

"Oh?" I looked my question at Simon, but it was Diane who answered, dropping the name almost carelessly from her full red lips.

"Jennifer Rumble."

"Isn't that the poor woman they found in the river?" Miss Simpson gasped. She wavered between shocked pleasure that she might be connected to tragedy, and concern that some scandal might accrue.

"You were the one who found her, weren't you?" Diane persisted. "Your name was in the paper."

"It must have been dreadful," Simon shook his head.

"I didn't know you knew her," I said to him. "You should

have said something."

"Was working up to it," he shrugged. "It's not the kind of thing you talk about lightly."

Diane ran one finger along a bookshelf, flicked her nails. "We were devastated of course. She was over at our house what, a week before it happened? And no warning at all. I keep thinking if we hadn't had to go south just then, she might have talked to us. Did you meet her? Were you able to talk to her?"

"Diane." Simon spoke her name in a tone both warning and reproving.

She bit her lip. The lipstick rubbed off on to her upper front teeth. She waved one hand distractedly, as if to dismiss the questions she was obviously bursting to ask.

"All right. Never mind."

Miss Simpson wedged herself between the two of them, clutching both by the arms. "Shall we go?" she chirped.

Diane shook herself free. She spoke to me, but her eyes were on Simon. "It's so sweet that you two have met up after all these years. You'll have so much to talk about, you must come to dinner. We move into the cottage on Friday, so one day next week. I'll call you. You're in the book?"

"And bring your husband, too, of course," Simon added.

"Will doesn't go out much," I said. "He's very busy."

"You'll come alone then." Diane clinched the matter. "I'll call you as soon as we're settled. Now, come on, Simon, Auntie Margaret is getting anxious."

"I'll see you," Simon said and in his mouth the words were full of promise.

I had no more sales that day. I sat on the stool, flipping through sales catalogues, brooding over the past. Simon had not wanted me then. What did he want with me now? Strangers brushed in and out of the store, none of them staying any longer than they needed to circle the shop, glancing at titles. Finally I began to shelve the books from the pile by the desk. I was arranging the children's section when Stephanie arrived.

"Sorry I'm late," she called.

"You are?" I looked at my watch. I should have been home by now, greeting Sadie, preparing lunch.

"The car wouldn't start again," she rushed on. "Then, when Alan came for the kids, Megan didn't want to go because she promised to play with Katie today and Alan won't let the kids bring friends to his apartment. Then Michael couldn't find his homework book and Ben insisted on taking his teddy, though Alan told him only babies need stuffed toys. Kids! You don't know how lucky you are."

"I didn't get the window changed," I said.

"It can wait. Has it been busy today?" She peered at the cash register tape.

"No, very quiet for a Saturday."

"Good. I brought my wools with me." She placed a red leather bag on the counter, and fished through it for a pamphlet which she thrust at me. "I'm embroidering new chair covers for the dining room suite. It was Alan's grandmother's you know and he never let me change them. I'm hoping to get them done for Christmas, but with the kids I don't have time to work at home."

She moved the book catalogues off the desk to make room for a large square of cloth and a collection of brightly coloured wool skeins.

"I haven't finished these either," I said, gesturing at the one row of books remaining on the floor.

"I'll get to them later." Stephanie pulled out the stool and sat down. I reached around her to sign the register tape to show that the receipt total balanced with the cash.

"By the way," she said, "what do you think of Dr. Long's latest idea?"

"I missed her the last time she came in," I answered. "When was it, yesterday?"

"No, it was two days ago. Haven't Karen and Lil said anything to you about it?"

"She's not closing the store?" That was my constant fear. I hated the idea of having to look for another job in this town. When I decided to get out of the house and find work, I hadn't wanted to go back into a library. There were no library jobs available anyway, especially for someone without an advanced degree. It seemed nowadays that even the simplest job required the right piece of paper to get in the door, that experience counted for nothing. The store, in spite of the low pay and shift work, satisfied my love for books while keeping me occupied with other people, and needs other than my own. I was convinced it wouldn't last.

"No. But she wants one of us to become manager. The good doctor is tired of making the trip up here all the time. She goes on holiday so often to Colorado or the Islands, she wants someone here to take on the responsibility of running the place." Stephanie paused to stroke the pleats of her long tartan kilt smoothly down over her knees. The silver oversized pin on her skirt matched the silver bracket of the cameo brooch that graced the right shoulder of her crisp white blouse. Her dark hair fit her like a close cap without curl or loose end. "Karen didn't say anything? I thought she'd be on about it to you right away."

"We haven't really had a chance to talk." I thought about it. "Makes a lot of sense, though. Who does she have in mind?"

Stephanie grimaced. "That's just it. She won't say. She wants us to decide who's to take charge. The idea is that once Karen finishes school and gets a teaching job, the manager will take on her shifts as well and the other two will split the remainder. So it'll mean more hours as well as more pay."

"And more responsibility."

"That too." She snipped a length of scarlet wool, held it to a needle against the light. "Lil Carver's been here longest, but of course she won't want the job."

"Why not?"

"I really don't think she's up to it. Besides, her husband wouldn't like it." Stephanie licked one end of the strand and knotted it tightly.

"What's he got to do with it?"

"Fred Carver doesn't approve of wives working outside the home. Do you think he'd stand for her being made the boss?"

"What choice would he have if she wants it?"

"Don't be so naive, Rosalie." She studied a diagram drawn on the cloth and began to make tiny stitches.

"Do you want the job?"

She glanced up at me, then turned her full attention to her work. "If I were asked, I wouldn't say no."

"I thought this was just a stop gap for you. Until the divorce is settled and you can move back to Ottawa."

"The kids don't want to move away."

Great, I thought to myself. I'd been looking forward to her leaving. She never did her share of the unpleasant jobs, the dusting of shelves, the vacuuming, the annual stock taking which came just after Christmas when, she always asserted, she was simply too exhausted to help.

Stephanie came to work in the store shortly after I did. She and Alan Thompson, a psychology professor at the university, were still married then. She needed a job she said, "not because of the money, but to give me something to do while the kids are in school." Now that she was separated, she talked about returning to her hometown where her parents could help out with the children while she looked for a permanent job at a government salary.

"Well," she said. "We're to talk it over together, and then discuss it with Dr. Long when she's next in town."

I nodded. "I'll speak to Karen and Lil."

"You don't have to." She put her work down. "I can talk to both of them and get the consensus. I suggested to Dr. Long that she and I have lunch when she next comes in. I'm on in the morning that day so it makes sense."

"I think we should all meet her together." I picked up my bag. "It's a decision that affects us all, so we should all be in on it. No secrets."

"I don't want the job, if that's what you're thinking." Stephanie tossed her head. "I'll do it if I'm asked, of course, but it's not what I want. I've got the best interests of all of us, and Dr. Long, in mind."

"Right," I said. "See you Thursday." And I left.

By the time Will got home from work, I was in bed, reading a new LeCarré. I heard Sadie's welcome, the closing of doors, thunk of tool case on the kitchen floor, footsteps on the stairs. Will went to the bathroom before he came into the bedroom, already undressing. Even after fifteen years, I like to watch him get ready for bed. He sleeps naked.

He put his watch on top of the dresser and sat heavily on the bed. "Bad day?" I asked. I put down my book and turned out the light. He stretched, one hand rubbing his face.

"Yeah. God, I'm so tired."

"You'll never guess what happened at the store today."

"Stephanie finally quit."

"If only. No, she told me that Dr. Long wants to make one of us manager. Of course, she thinks she's the one should have the job, forget that Lil's worked there longer than any of us and that I've been there longer than her."

"Won't Dr. Long make that decision for herself?"

"No chance. She believes we should cooperate, decide among ourselves. I talked to Karen about it. Not much will change except that Dr. Long will only come in a couple of times a year and the manager will have to keep the accountant up to date, maintain the schedule of work, that sort of thing. There'll be more hours to work and a pay raise."

"Do you want to do it?"

"I don't think so."

"You seem kind of bored lately."

"I think Lil should have it and so does Karen. Now we just have to persuade her to ask for it. Even Stephanie wouldn't have the nerve to stand in her way."

"And if Lil won't take it, what will you do then?"

"I'll have to think about that. It means a commitment to work there much longer than I thought I would."

"You've been there three years already."

"I know. But there's always the chance that something more interesting will turn up. I can't see myself working part time for the rest of my life. Working for someone else. I'm tired of having to be polite to whoever walks into the store and of having to deal with salesmen who are barely out of their teens, but think they know everything there is to know about books and women."

"Someone in particular giving you a hard time?"

"The Reverend came in today."

Will made a noise, part grunt, part murmur. I took it for interest.

"So did a guy I knew in high school, Simon Harper. His wife's the Pink Lady's niece. You remember me telling you about Miss Simpson? Anyway, the Harpers are moving into the Simpson cottage up on Mud Lake for a few weeks. They invited us to dinner."

"When?"

"Next week sometime."

"You know I hate that kind of thing, all that remembering so-and-so stuff. Reunions."

"I know. I said you probably wouldn't come, but I think I'll go. It might be interesting to see how the other half lives."

"They rich?"

"He was telling me about his houses and cars. He drives a Triumph, a real beauty. They have a travel agency, trips to exotic places, that kind of thing. You could talk to them about some of the places you're planning to visit on our round-the-world odyssey."

Will groaned. "Another reason to beg off. Talking about going away only makes it harder to keep on slogging at work. Do you mind? I'll come if you want me to."

"No it's all right. I think I'd rather go alone."

"You know this guy well? You've never said much about him."

"Nothing to tell." A kiss on a beach, so long ago. "They knew Jennifer Rumble."

Will caught his breath. "Really?" he asked, his voice almost steady. "Well?"

"She and Diane were good friends. Apparently she was at their house just before she died. They were away when it happened, so didn't get to the funeral. Simon didn't want to talk about her, but I got the feeling that Diane was anxious to hear all the details." I shivered. "I hope not. I still have dreams about finding her body. I don't want to go through describing that again."

"Maybe you shouldn't go."

"I've already said I would. Besides it'll be fun to talk about high school again. I wonder who Simon has kept up with?"

"I have to go to sleep, Rosie, I'm beat." Will yawned and curled into a ball, his usual sleeping position.

"Goodnight then."

"Goodnight."

We both lay silent, back to back. I practiced deep breathing, forcing my limbs to relax, one by one, as if by doing so I could trick myself into dreamless sleep.

"Are you asleep?" Will touched my arm. I shook myself out of a doze that may have lasted minutes or hours. It was still dark. I turned towards him, seeing only a black mask backlit by the glow of the streetlight.

"No. What time is it?"

"About two-thirty."

"What's wrong?"

"I've been so busy lately," he said. "I know I haven't been paying enough attention to you. I'm sorry."

"It's all right."

"It's not all right. I just don't know what I can do about it. It wasn't supposed to be this way with us. We were always going to have time to talk to each other, do things together. Moving up here, starting the business . . ."

"Things are going well for you," I said. "You've got more jobs than you can handle. Remember how we worried when we first came, that you wouldn't get enough work? Then it was either feast or famine. Now it's all feast."

"It's the nature of the business."

"But we knew that before we started." I rolled over on to my back. "Aren't you happy? Happier than when you were working in government?"

"It's not that I'm not happy. I like the work. I like to be able to do what I want to do, and do well by it. It's just that there never seems to be a break when I need it. When we both need it."

"Don't worry." I reached over to stroke his face, feeling the lines smooth out beneath my hand. "If I could help . . ."

"You help by being here with me. For me." After a moment, he added, "I was talking to Kirsten Loring today about her kitchen renovation. She and her husband are our age, both teachers at Central High. They've not been able to have kids either, but have adopted a baby from somewhere in Central America. They're hoping to have her home for Christmas."

"So you do still want to adopt?" I sniffed back sudden tears. "I thought we'd decided to wait, to let nature take its course."

"We can't keep waiting forever," he said. "I want a son. Or a daughter, it doesn't matter which. Someone to take to ball games and music lessons. Watch him learn to talk and read and ride a bike. Grow up." He turned to hug me. "I want to be a father, Rosie," he said, his voice muffled by my hair, his breath hot against my cheek. "A better father than my old man, but a father."

"My period's late again," I said, fighting to keep my voice steady, the useless crying at bay.

He dropped his arms. "How long?"

"Just a couple of days."

He groaned. "We've been through this so many times before."

"But this time it's different. I just know it is."

"Have you taken your temperature?"

"It's low. But it's early yet."

We lay still, silent. After two years of fertility counselling, trying drugs that did nothing but prolong the agony of waiting five weeks, six weeks, seven weeks for bleeding to begin, I had come to rely only on the basal body thermometer. Each time my period was late, I took my temperature. No matter how ill I felt, it stayed low. Within days the period would begin. Even now, I hoped each time that a miracle would happen, that the waiting would go on and on and on and end with a baby.

Will shifted away from me. "Maybe we should begin the process for adopting, talk to an agency. The paperwork takes a long time and the anticipation might just trigger something."

"I don't want someone else's baby. I want my own."

"What about going back to the clinic, trying that again? It's been a few years, they've got new drugs, new procedures."

"I refuse to be a medical guinea pig. Remember what it was like the last time, we had no privacy, no intimacy, doctors poking around all the time. And after all that, nothing happens anyway."

"You're thirty-eight," he said. "I'm forty. How long can we wait?"

"I just couldn't do it."

"Okay, it's your body, your decision. But think about it,

will you? There are babies in the world that need parents as much as we need a baby." He rolled over. "I've got to get some sleep."

I lay and listened to the sound of his breath, trying to match my own pulse to it. My breasts ached. I thought about a baby, the small hands, the delicate blue veins of its head. Usually I kept my longing at bay with concentration on work, with the endless chores of fixing up an old house. What had I done to deserve this sorrow? Why was I barren? I turned my pillow over again. Will began to snore. I thought about getting out of the warm bed, going downstairs to read where the light would not bother him, where Sadie would keep me company.

Car headlights swept across the room. Our house was on a cul de sac ending in the park. Sometimes teenagers parked by the entrance gates to drink, neck, smoke dope. The police kept a regular patrol going by and I thought this might be one of their cars. The engine purred loudly in the stillness of the night, a giant cat on the prowl. A door slammed and I heard running feet, muffled laughter, a loud thud as something hit the porch.

Sadie erupted in a frenzy of barking that nearly drowned the sound of squealing tires. I scrambled to open the blind, but was in time only to see red lights fading down the hill. Will shrugged on his robe as he raced down the stairs, yelling at the dog to be quiet.

FOUR

I held on to Sadie. She quivered with excitement, gasping high-pitched yips. Will turned the deadbolt, then stepped back, flinging the door open.

A small fire flamed in the draft. Will picked up the rubber door mat and slapped until all that was left were a few tattered rags stinking of oily smoke. He kicked the mess off the porch into the shadows beside the concrete stoop.

"What was that?" I asked.

"Kids and their pranks." He went down the steps and peered up the street. It was dead quiet, deserted.

"Our house could have caught fire." I shivered and pulled my robe tighter.

"It might be those boys you caught last week vandalizing the willows. Didn't you tell them you were going to report them? Maybe this is their way of retaliating."

"Should we call the cops?"

"Not much point. There's no message and neither of us saw the car. There's nothing for the police to investigate." He turned the rags over with a stick, spreading them apart along the path. "Nothing left. Let's go back to bed."

We lay in silence, each on our own side of the bed. It was hard to believe that children were capable of such malice, though I recalled too clearly the sullen looks on those boys' faces when I yelled at them about stripping green branches from the trees. With their ripped blue jeans and leather jackets, slicked hair and cigarettes, they aped the bad boys I remembered from my early teens. Did they know where I lived? Would they be satisfied with their small fire, with this scare?

Will hugged me. "Stop worrying," he whispered. "It was just a stupid joke."

He kissed my cheek and I turned fully to face him, my arms pulling him closer. Afterwards, we lay still until our breaths separated. We sighed at the same moment as our bodies returned to their usual isolation.

By the time I finished showering the next morning, Will was sipping his second cup of coffee. I put my arms around him, laid my head against his back. "I'm not working next Saturday," I said. "Let's go away for the weekend, down to the city, see a few movies. We could ask Karen to take care of Sadie and go for the whole day, spend some time in the bookstores, and eat out somewhere special."

"Sounds good."

I dropped my arms. I'd heard that tone of voice before. "But what?"

"Didn't I tell you about that developer, Luke Marbella, who wants to build himself a house with quote character unquote? His wife saw the work I did for the Debarons and wants me to do their kitchen. It could lead to a lot of business, a steady line of jobs. I have to go out to their building site on Friday and finish up the plans with them on Saturday. I thought you might want to go to the movies with Karen."

"I don't want to go out with Karen. She's my best friend, not my husband. Why didn't you tell me about this before?

"Because every time I mention a new job, you go into your martyred wife act."

"What is that supposed to mean?"

Will stood up, pushing his chair back so roughly that it almost fell. "I don't want to get into this now. It's bad enough having to spend Sunday working, without getting into a fight first thing."

"That's it, then?"

He looked at me without speaking. Lines around his mouth had pulled his lips into a permanent frown. Blue shadows bruised his eyes. All night, on the edge of my dreams of fire and smoke, I was aware of him tossing, his smothered groans. I wanted, needed, to hug him again and stepped forward just as he turned to grab his coat from the hall rack.

"We'll talk tonight," he said. Then, "Damn, I've got Jerry coming in to help with the Martin cabinets. It's the only time he's got free this week. If I get this Marbella contract, I'll be able to hire him full time. As it is, he's got two other guys he works for. I have to use his help when I can get it."

"Never mind," I said. "We can go to the city another weekend."

"Sorry."

He stood before the half open door in the hall. I stayed in the living room. The few feet of space between us crackled with tension.

"Bye." He was gone. It was some ten minutes or so before I moved.

In the kitchen, coffee still bubbled on the ring. I dumped it, watched the black whirlpool disappear down the drain.

The phone rang. I stretched out to it, and overbalanced. I grabbed the counter to keep myself from falling. One hand knocked the receiver flying. I picked it up.

"Hello?"

Silence.

"Hello?" I nearly shouted this time.

There was a noise, a snicker or a groan, then a click. The dial tone buzzed.

We often get wrong numbers, I told myself. I hung up, then picked it up again immediately. I didn't want it to ring. I called

Karen instead.

"What time is it?" she moaned when she finally answered.

"Almost noon. Well, nine-thirty. Did you have a late night?"

"If only. After the market yesterday, Mom wanted to drive out to the cemetery to visit Dad, then we had to stop by Aunt Ellen's. By the time we got out of there, it was supper time and Mom insisted on treating me to dinner at Swiss Chalet. I figured the night was shot, so suggested we go see *Driving Miss Daisy* which that new repertory cinema is showing again. That, of course, led to tears. I wish she'd stop begging me to move home. I like this place."

Karen's flat was in an old building near the courthouse downtown. I could see her lounging in her waterbed, red phone tucked under one ear while she searched for cigarettes and her lighter. A snap, a deep intake of breath, a long sigh told me she'd found them among the clutter of books and papers that character-ized every surface of her life.

"I thought you were quitting?" I asked her.

"Just putting this out," she said. "Wait a minute." I could hear church bells, the singsong of a fire siren. "All I need is one puff to start the day."

"Sure."

"What are you calling for, anyway? Not just to get on my case about smoking?"

"No. I forgot to tell you who came in the store yesterday. The Reverend dropped by with his usual rant. And then a blast from the past: Simon Harper."

"The guitar player?"

"The very one. He's married to the Pink Lady's niece of all people. Her name's Diane Simpson. Did you ever know her? She grew up here apparently. They're going to stay up at the lake for a few weeks, on holiday. At this time of year!"

"Diane Simpson," she said. "I remember her from high

school, I think. Tall and blonde? She used to speak in a British accent because her family lived in England for a year. They moved to Toronto. I think her Dad works for an insurance company or something like that."

"That's right. She doesn't have the accent any more but you wouldn't believe the clothes."

Karen laughed. "Now tell me about him? What's he like?"

"Nice."

"Did you recognize him?"

"Not at first. After all, we didn't know each other that well. His cousin was really my friend."

"Isn't this the famous Simon, the romance on the beach?"

"You know too much."

"You talk too much. What does Will think of him turning up?"

"What's to think? He's too busy to care." I sighed.

"Come off it, Rosie," Karen warned. "That's not fair to Will."

"He was late getting in last night. Again. We didn't have much of a chance to talk. But they've invited me out to the lake for dinner next week."

"Wish I could be a fly on the wall."

"I wish Will would come too. He's so busy all the time."

"You're lucky to have him. You have no idea what it's like to be single, trying to find a decent date in this town. All the guys I meet are married or gay or only out for a good time. Or they're totally committed to their mothers. Will's a really good man. You've got history together. Remember when we all met back in college? Those were the days."

"Those days were a long time ago."

"But it's only work, right? You knew when he went into business for himself that he was going to have to work real hard."

I wound the phone cord around one finger, then another. "Sometimes it's like we've been caught in one of those old movies, a fifties time warp. He's the Man of the House, slaving at his business, working all hours to buy the Little Woman everything her heart desires. He's doing what he's always wanted to do. He gets to meet lots of people and though he's working for them, he's also working for himself. And me, I'm Hannah Housewife, mop in one hand, cookbook in the other."

"Hannah Housewife!" she spluttered. "That's the last thing I'd call you. If my mother saw the condition of your coffee table, she'd have a fit."

"You know what I mean." I felt so miserable that none of her joking could cheer me up. Besides, the living room wasn't all that messy. I'd been in worse. Somewhere.

"Okay." After a pause, she continued, "I'm only asking this because I'm your friend, you realize. Are you having problems in bed? Is that the trouble?"

I managed a laugh. "No, it's not that. In fact, it's almost too good. Instead of talking, we have sex."

"I can think of worse things. Like chastity."

"But I'm so confused, Karen. Will's talking about adoption again. You know I'm desperate to have a baby of our own, but I know it's not going to happen. And then I think, well, maybe it's not meant to be, maybe I should be looking for some kind of real work to do. I'm almost forty. I've got no pension, no profession to rely on if something happens to Will. And I hate being so dependent on him."

"What about being bookstore manager?"

"It's still part-time, with no security. What if Dr. Long decided the store was too much trouble and wanted to sell it? We couldn't afford to buy and I'd be out of a job. I've been there three years and when I look at the time I don't know where it's gone, and I don't know what I've done. I feel my life is drifting away."

"You're not helpless." I heard the telltale gasp of breath. Karen had lit another cigarette. "What do you want to do?"

"All I know is what I don't want to do: I don't want to go

back to the doctors, I don't want to adopt, I don't want to go back to the library, I don't want to work for such little pay."

"Sounds like all you do want is to find the meaning of life."

"Meaning for my life," I answered. After a moment, we both laughed. "Seriously," I went on, "I feel as confused now as when I was in high school. I thought all these questions got solved automatically after thirty?"

"Maybe you should talk to someone, get some help."

"A shrink?"

"Don't be so quick to dismiss the idea. You know how much Marianne has helped me. I could get you an appointment to see her if you want."

"No, I don't need that yet. I'm just down today. Will and I sort of had a fight this morning."

"I gathered that. What about?"

"Oh, the usual. He works too much."

"And you don't have enough to keep you busy. I wish I could say the same. I've got three term papers due by the end of the month and half the readings are missing from the library. Now there's a job for you."

I took her opening to get away from questions about my marriage. "How is school going? Are you happy?"

"There's a lot of bureaucracy, of course. And it's tough to be with kids half my age, who haven't done any living at all, and think they know everything and can teach anything. But I do love being in the classroom."

"You're so lucky."

"Lucky? Me?" Karen sighed. "If my mother heard you say that, she'd die laughing."

"You've got your own life, your own place. You've got a future planned out. You know what you're doing."

"I'd trade you any day." Another quick intake of breath. "I get pretty lonely."

"Are you happy you came back? Or do you find you miss

the west coast?"

"I miss some of my friends, there, yeah. But with all the cutbacks and without more training, I couldn't be sure of keeping my counselling work. And the people I had to deal with, the women and kids in abuse centres, it was pretty depressing. I think it was one of the reasons I couldn't stay with any man, I kept seeing those bruises."

"You never told me that. Was Jake violent?"

"No, it wasn't that any guy I lived with was like that. But there was always the potential, if you see what I mean. When Dad died and Mom needed me home, it seemed like a good idea to turn my life around. My therapist has helped too. I get frightened sometimes."

"You can always talk to me."

"A real source of strength." Karen laughed, a little shakily. "My, we're a fine pair, we two."

I listened to the hum on the wire, stared out at clouds sweeping across the forested hill framed in the window. It was time to change this subject too.

"So what's it like to be in a room full of ten-year-olds?"

"Let me tell you." And she was off.

We talked about her pupils and the other student teachers for almost an hour. I don't know why I didn't tell her about the fire. It seemed so bizarre, so far removed from the world of chalk dust and playground rivalries. When we finally hung up, I went out and picked up the sodden rags, stuffed them into a large green plastic bag and dropped it in the garbage pail. The metal lid fit badly. I banged it shut. Out of sight, out of mind. There were skid marks turning the corner of our street, deep ruts where a car had parked on the soft shoulder. I wondered when and how long it had sat there.

I spent the morning doing chores, the usual Sunday clean-up. After lunch, I went upstairs to my study. It was a small room with the high sloped ceiling characteristic of this Edwardian house, plain white walls, varnished pine floor. A big desk faced the dormer window which looked out over the apple trees in our side yard to the maples in the park. With the leaves gone, I could see the river and an arrow of geese on their way south. I owed Annie a letter. I had Will's accounts to update. I sat for an hour, staring at blank paper. In the end, I decided to take Sadie for a walk.

Although a light rain was falling, I headed for the river. I hadn't been that way since finding the body, but I was too restless to walk city streets. Sadie wriggled with delight while I dressed in anorak and boots, found her leash, and locked the doors behind us. As soon as we were through the gates, I let her loose. She raced in wide circles, nose close to the ground, tail wagging. I picked up a straight sturdy branch that had fallen from one of the old trees, and followed her, swishing at milkweed pods as I passed.

The river reflected the steel gray sky. The rain hissed as it hit the water. Sadie didn't go in, but stood on a bit of pebbly beach, looking up and down for birds. The footbridge was deserted. I decided to walk up to the hydro dam to see the waterfall whose roar drowned the faint noise of traffic on the streets downtown. The trail along the river bank would be too muddy; I headed out along the top of the bluff, calling the dog as I went. The weather depressed her and, her early exuberance dampened, she walked quietly at my heel.

A small copse of poplar and birch clung to the cliff above the sluices where water rushed white and frothing. Sadie took off after a rabbit and disappeared into the trees.

The noise was tremendous, exhilarating. A stiff breeze blew off the river and pulled my hood away from my hair. I raised my face to the mist, eyes closed, shoulders slumped, arms hanging loose at my sides. I thought about Will, in bed, last night. Each time like the first time. I grinned. We used to spend whole days in bed, taking turns to bring in snacks from the kitchen, the bedside table littered with plates and bottles and overflowing

ashtrays. When my mother called, I would listen to her complaints, one hand on my mouth to stifle laughter, the other trying
to push Will away. "I have to go," I would say. "I'll call you later."

"What's wrong?" she always answered. "Why don't you
come home from university this weekend? You haven't taken a
break from study in ages. You could bring that young man with
you, what's his name, Will something. Isn't it about time I met
him?"

Even after we married in a ceremony orchestrated for her
friends, my mother ghastly pale in her flowered silk mother-of-
the-bride gown, I never had time for her gossip and grievances.
Marrying Will was not only a sop to her conventionality, but my
escape from that house of illness and death. She went into the
hospital while we were on our honeymoon, and never came back
home. Now I wished for my mother to hold me, comfort me from
fears as vague as the night demons that slept under my childhood
bed.

Thinking of those days, I needed suddenly to hear Will's
voice, to talk to him even about the weather, even over the phone,
even though he could not get home for hours. I turned to call the
dog and faced a stranger.

"Don't scream," he said.

I swallowed my cry. "I was going to call my dog."

"Don't." He glanced around. Sadie was still in the bushes,
rooting for rabbits. "I don't like dogs."

He was a small man, as short as I was and very thin. His
black hair hung in wet ribbons that seeped into the turned-up
collar of his suit jacket. His nose was red with cold, a drop of water
trembling at its tip; his eyes seemed unnaturally large and green
under a thick bar of bushy eyebrows. He was shaved so cleanly
that no shadow softened the lines of his jaw and high cheekbones.
His pant legs were soaked, a few weeds trailing from the cuffs,
his feet pinched in patent shoes splattered with mud. He must
have been down at the water's edge. I couldn't imagine why

anyone would climb down there dressed in a business suit and in this sort of weather. He picked off a burr that clung to his sleeve.

"So we meet at last." He expected me to recognize him.

"I'm sorry," I said. "I don't know who you are and I don't talk to strangers."

He stepped closer, raising one hand. I flinched and he smiled, a thinning of pale lips. "You are Rosalie Cairns. You live at 63 Park Road. You're married to William Cairns, a carpenter, and you have no children. You work part-time in a bookstore. You arranged a meeting with Jennifer Rumble and she gave you a file and her diary the last time she came here. I want them."

"What are you talking about? How do you know so much about me?"

He grinned. "The papers, please?"

"I never met her. She was dead when I found her. And I don't have any papers from her either."

"So, it was just coincidence you were walking by the river that day?"

"Yes, it was."

"And the cops just happened to overlook her briefcase when they found her clothes and her car? Simon Harper came into your bookstore simply by chance?"

"What's Simon got to do with this?"

"He was her partner, of course. One of them."

"They were friends. Simon and his wife and Jennifer."

He sneered. "I suppose you're going to tell me next that your husband used to meet her all those times just to talk business? In candlelit restaurants?"

"That's enough. Leave me alone." I threw the stick at him, turned and began to run, calling for Sadie. I heard him curse as he slipped on the wet grass, but I dared not slow down. Sadie burst out of the woods and raced after me, snapping at my heels, thinking this was a game. When I reached the gate, I looked back. The man had given up the chase. He stood quite still, staring after me, his hands held up to his eyes. Something flashed in the weak light. Binoculars or a camera. I hurried home, putting the chain on the door behind me.

"Did he touch you? Did he threaten you, physically or verbally?" Constable Finlay asked. He was the detective who investigated Rumble's death, the only person I could think to phone, who might help.

"He raised his hand." I could almost hear the sigh. "He knew everything about me, where I live, where I work, my husband's name. He knew Will had met her years ago."

"Your husband knew Ms. Rumble?"

"He met her once. But that guy even knew that I knew Simon Harper. He must be watching me."

"Who's Harper?"

"His cousin's an old friend of mine. He dropped into the store the other day, quite out of the blue. He knew Jennifer Rumble, and so did his wife. But that man said they were partners."

"Harper's a lawyer?"

"No, he owns a travel company."

"So what's the connection?"

"I don't know. It's your job to find out. And I want you to keep him away from me."

"I'll send a car down to look around. He's probably long gone by now. I'm sure he was just some crank, somebody who read about you finding the body in the paper. There're a lot of weirdos out there, you know. People who get off on death, especially violent death, whether it was suicide or not. He probably got his thrills putting a scare into you. You won't see him again."

"But he was very insistent about those papers."

"There were no papers." It was almost a question.

"There's something else." I took a deep breath. "I answered

the phone a while ago: there were no words, just some heavy breathing. And someone set a fire on our porch last night."

"What?"

"Someone threw a clump of rags on the porch and set fire to them. We didn't see anyone, but we heard the car."

"Why didn't you say anything about this earlier?"

"I don't know. We thought it might be kids. A sort of late Hallowe'en joke."

This time Finlay's sigh blew along the wire. "You should have called last night."

I shrugged. Silence hummed along the line.

"Well," he said at last, "I'll make sure the patrols keep an eye out for anything suspicious. Maybe you should stay away from the river for awhile. Go on a holiday."

"I should just forget all about this, right?" I sneered. "Pretend nothing happened?"

"I know this has been an upsetting time for you." He kept his tone measured and even, a doctor giving a patient the bad news. "Finding a body like that is enough to put fear into anyone and nuts, like that guy in the park, are always scary. But the fire and the phone call could be coincidence, no connection with this other business at all. As for Ms. Rumble's death, it looks like suicide for sure, but we are investigating. If anything comes up, I'll let you know right away. But you stay out of it now. You're a witness, pure and simple, a bystander. You take care of your life and I'll do my job and take care of the corpse, okay?"

"Okay."

"You call me if anything else happens."

"I will."

"Take care, then." He hung up the phone.

I leaned against the fridge. Finlay's argument made sense. I should keep out of his way. I should get on with my life.

That man in the park had no right to threaten me. I was sure he was involved somehow with the fire and the phone call. I was tired of being frightened and alone. I was angry too, at Jennifer Rumble for killing herself in my river, at the fate that had led me to find her, at Finlay for his fatherly advice which, even if sage, was certainly unwanted. I picked up the phone again and dialled Will. He listened to my story without comment.

"He said that you knew Jennifer Rumble, that she was a friend of yours."

Will coughed. "I told you that I met her. Once. Years ago."

"He implied that you knew her well. That you used to meet her in restaurants. Often."

"He was lying."

"He claimed that her briefcase was missing. He wanted to know if we had it."

"Why would we have her stuff?" Will's voice had that edge to it I recognized. He would be drumming his fingers on the desk, one foot tapping the floor.

"That's just it. I don't know. Neither do the cops."

"You told them I knew her?"

"Is it a secret?"

"No, of course not." He paused. "Believe me, Rosie, I hardly knew the woman. We had some business dealings a long time ago when I worked in the Immigration Department. I told you and Karen that after she was identified, remember? I hadn't talked to her in years. I didn't think such a chance acquaintance was worth telling the police about."

"Your wife finds the corpse of someone you knew well a few years ago and you didn't think it important to tell the police that?"

"I didn't know her well, I keep telling you. It was business."

"Is that why she really came to town? To see you?"

"What are you trying to say, Rosie? Don't you believe me?"

I leaned my forehead on the refrigerator. It shivered and hummed.

"Rosie?" Will asked again. "Are you still there?"

"Yes."

"Do you want me to come home now?"

I pictured him sitting at the cluttered desk in the corner of his workshop that he called his office, his fingers combing his hair back away from his face. Underlining his silence was the distant whine of an electric saw, the chatter of a radio talk show. He would sit leaning forward, one elbow planted on a stack of paper covered with graphic designs and rows of figures. While he spoke into the telephone, he would be staring at his computer, the cursor pulsing on the blank screen.

"Yes," I whispered.

"As soon as I can," he said. And then, "You know I love you."

I could hear the weariness in his voice.

FIVE

Finlay himself dropped by to see us that evening. A big man, balding and overweight, he looked much older than his forty years. He crouched to greet Sadie when I answered the door. "Mind if I come in?"

"No. We've just finished supper. Would you like coffee or tea?"

He shook his head. "I'm on my way home myself. Just thought I'd check with you, see if there's anything else you might remember about Ms. Rumble."

I stood back and watched him straighten up. He dusted off the pants of his blue suit, shifted his shoulders to ease the jacket. His shirt was a pale blue cotton unbuttoned at the neck. A red tie trailed from one pocket. I imagined his gun in its leather holster, a second cold heart still in the hollow beneath his left arm.

"Nice dog," he said.

Sadie grinned at him, her tail thumping the floor. Not too many visitors were willing to greet her at eye level. She clearly adored him.

"Do you have a dog?" I asked.

"Used to," he answered. His eyes swept the hall, not missing any detail: the worn runner covering the varnished boards, the church windowframe transformed into a mirror, the silky wood of the stripped bannisters. He ran one hand along the rail. "Nice job. Who did it?"

"I did. A while ago. Shows you what a little frustration can do when you put it to work."

My joke fell flat.

"Is your husband home?"

Will slouched into the living room. He said nothing, simply stood there as if waiting, head bent and shoulders slumped. If you didn't know him well, you might think he was guilty, trying to hide something. To me, it was just shyness coupled with his distrust of uniformed authority ingrained in the wild days of student revolt and experiments with illegal substances.

"Perhaps we could have a word in private?" Finlay said to him.

Will shrugged and jerked his head towards the dining room. He didn't wait to see who would follow, but began sifting through the papers spread over the table. He picked up his coffee cup, then put it back down without sipping.

"You have to excuse him," my voice was not much louder than a whisper. "He's terribly overworked."

"No problem," Finlay smiled and walked in after him. I hesitated a moment before going upstairs to my study where I sat staring at bills while their voices rumbled below me, too muffled for me to hear what was being said. Once I heard a loud thump as if someone had struck the table, then the telltale creak of floorboards as someone paced.

Finlay didn't stay long. He shouted a good-bye up the stairs as he let himself out the door. I met Will in the hall.

"He thinks you need a holiday," he said. He fingered the delicate wood carving on the newel post. I sat on the stair just out of his reach. He didn't look up.

"What do you think?" I challenged.

"It's not such a bad idea. Maybe you should think about going down to the city for a few days. Visit the library, see how everyone's doing. You haven't seen Marci in weeks, and you used to be such good friends."

"You want to get rid of me."

"That's not true and you know it. Ever since you found that body, you've been nervous, on edge. A break will do you good. You should get away until all this blows over."

"What about Sadie?"

"She'll cope. I can walk her when I get home from work."

"What about my job?"

"You could take vacation."

"Not on such short notice, in the Christmas season."

"Well, it's up to you." He sighed.

"What did he want to talk to you about?"

"Just details about my relationship with Jennifer Rumble. Such as it was. And whether I'd heard from her before her death. I told him the truth. I barely knew her and hadn't talked to her in years. He, at least, believes me."

I turned to go back upstairs. "I'm going to read in bed for awhile."

"Sure. And what about going away?"

"I'll think about it."

After that, Will took over the job of walking the dog. I rode the bus to work, avoiding the footbridge and the park. We couldn't talk about anything, not even shopping lists, without accusations and acrimony, each small disagreement ballooning beyond the particular event to include every sore point of each other's behaviour. It was a relief when Diane Harper phoned to invite us to dinner. I agreed to go, alone.

As usual, that evening began with another argument, this time over the car. At six o'clock it was pitch dark, a blustery night without a moon. I wanted to leave early to follow the directions Diane had given me. There would be no streetlights out at the lake, and I feared I wouldn't recognize the turn-off to the cottage.

Will sat at the dining room table, finishing the cheese omelette he had cooked for himself.

"How do I look?" I asked, turning so he could view my new

red corduroy skirt and Fair Isle patterned sweater. I wore boots but carried shoes in one hand. "Have you seen my keys?"

"About the car," he answered. "I have to go back to the shop tonight to finish the Marbella plans on the computer. Why don't I drop you off? You can get a ride home with someone else, or give me a call and I'll come get you."

I stopped rummaging through the bureau drawer that always collected pens, papers, scissors, scotch tape, perhaps keys. "I told you I needed the car tonight. I won't be fetched like a schoolgirl on a date."

"There's sure to be someone else there."

"They don't know anyone else in town except for Miss Simpson and I doubt very much she'll be there. From the way Diane spoke, I think it's supposed to be a quiet dinner, just the three of us. I told you I needed the car."

"You always drink too much wine," he attacked.

"You think I'm a drunk, that I'll smash up that precious car of yours?"

"That's not what I meant."

"If you're worried about me driving, why didn't you say you'd come? You were invited."

"I know you're a good driver," he countered. "It's not your control I'm concerned about. You know how dangerous that highway is on Saturday nights, people driving home from the bars. Besides it looks like it might snow, and the snow tires aren't on yet."

"I've driven in winter before." I found the keys among the seashells in a glass bowl on the windowsill.

"What about my work? The program I need to finish those graphics is on my office computer. I can't do it at home."

"I'll drop you off, it's on my way. You can take a bus back."

"Thanks. I'll freeze to death waiting for it."

"Maybe one of your customers will see you there and take pity. Maybe you should call one of them up, that girl I saw you talking to before you met me in the store last week. The brunette with the long legs."

"That was the Martin's daughter. She's still in high school, for goodness sake. If one of us is looking for adventure, it isn't me." He stood with such force that his chair toppled behind him. "When am I supposed to find the time for fooling around — if I wanted to fool around." He stormed into the hall, came back with his coat. "Let's go if we're going."

I followed him out to the garage. He sat in the driver's seat, fingers tapping on the wheel. He looked up at me. "I'll drive as far as my shop."

I got in the passenger's side. The Accord was the first car we had ever bought brand new. Will kept it immaculate, with the windshield washed inside and out, the finish waxed and shining. He slammed a tape into the deck and music erupted as the car lurched down the drive into the street. We didn't speak until we reached his shop. I got out and circled around to the other side. Will stood still, holding the door open. His breath steamed.

"I'm sorry," he said. "We always seem to be fighting."

I nodded.

"Drive carefully, won't you?"

"Worried about your car?"

"Worried about you."

I looked at him then. The wind tossed his hair back from his forehead which wrinkled with cold and concern. I touched his hand where it rested on the roof. "I'll be all right."

"Have a nice time." He kissed me, on the cheek.

"Don't wait up." I bent to get in the car but he caught me, hands on my arms, pulling me up, my face lifting to his.

"I do love you," he said, and we kissed long and hard as the first snow began to fall.

"I know," I finally replied.

The cottage was upriver about twenty miles, on a stretch of water that widened sufficiently to be called Mud Lake. The area had been developed to accommodate executive retirement homes among the venerable cottages which lined a gravel road that snaked from the highway down to the shore. The house I was looking for was a handsome two-storey wood frame cabin with a red shingle roof. It was set back from the road behind a grove of birch trees and a high cedar hedge. The gate had been left open for me; there were no other tracks on the drive that circled the yard.

When I got out of the car, I could smell woodsmoke and heard music that burst out of the house as Simon came to meet me. "Welcome," he cried.

I waved my bottle of wine.

He wore a red down vest over blue jeans. When he laughed, sweeping his arms in a gesture that took in the yard, the house, and the falling snow, the vest opened to show a soft denim shirt unbuttoned at the neck. "Isn't this weather great? There's nothing more exciting than the first winter storm. That's the problem with the south: no seasons. Come and see the lake. It's not frozen over yet."

An open verandah wrapped round the house. At the back, stairs the width of the porch led down to a lawn that sloped gently to the shore. A flagstaff stood pointed and white above a long low building. "Boat shed," said Simon as if he knew where I was looking.

Beyond it a line of rocks formed a black scalloped edge. I could hear the whisper of small waves breaking on the shore but could see the lake only as a darker movement rolling against the dark. In the light from the windows behind us, the snow fell in huge, soft flakes that melted on my face as they landed.

Simon touched my hair. "Looks like you're wearing a veil," he said. "Such delicate lace."

The kitchen door swung open and Diane appeared framed in the bright light, steamy garlic and drum beats eddying around her. Simon dropped his hand. She looked from me to him and back again. "So good to see you," she spoke formally. "Won't you come in?"

I looked back at the lake. I thought for a moment that something moved down by the boat shed, a shadow among the rocks. I shook away the illusion as I shook the snowflakes from my head.

Once inside, my glasses misted with the heat so there were a few minutes of confusion — coats and boots taken off, shoes put on, tissues found to clear the lenses — before I could properly examine the house.

The first floor was one big open room, divided by a counter top between kitchen and living area and by strategic placement of a sectional sofa and a long low table covered with magazines and bowls of silk flowers. Primitive oils graced the walls between uncurtained windows. Rag rugs and a couple of sheepskins were scattered over the pine floors. A polar bear fur complete with head stretched before a woodstove that squatted against the far wall with its black pipe rising to the high raftered ceiling. The kitchen was very modern, including even a microwave oven, but I was glad to see the pots simmering on the stove.

"I hope you don't mind spaghetti," said Diane. "It's Simon's specialty."

She uncorked the wine and poured it into three tall glasses. "Cheers." She clinked her glass to mine. "Come and sit down while Simon finishes up."

He was already busy at the stove, dipping a wooden spoon into one of the pots, his eyes closed while he considered the flavour. He sighed and then grinned at me. "Perfection, if I do say so myself."

"In here," Diane gestured towards the other room.

I followed her, choosing to sit on the sofa while she sank into a nest of patchwork pillows that cushioned the varnished maple of a spool rocker. She wrapped a flowered, fringed shawl around her shoulders.

"It's so cold tonight," she said.

"The fire's warm." I gestured to the woodstove whose flames glinted through the grate.

"I wanted to turn the propane heater on too. Simon wouldn't let me. He's such a perfectionist about such things. He'll even get up in the middle of the night to keep the fire going. I mean, really, there's no need for roughing it. He doesn't mind using the hot water or the toilet, I'll say that for him. Thank goodness Aunt Margaret had the outhouse torn down a few years ago, or who knows what that man might have insisted on."

I smiled uneasily. It was hot enough at this end of the room to make me wish I had chosen a shirt rather than sweater to wear. Diane was perfectly comfortable in a loose cotton blouse of flaming red that matched her long earrings. She wore black tights and black slippers without socks. Her eyes were heavily shadowed with blue, her lipstick and nail polish matched the brilliance of her shirt. Even the three rings she wore had red stones in them. Her blonde curls were in careful disarray. She leaned forward to pick up a jade cigarette box from the cedar chest that served as a coffee table. Her breasts swung with the movement and I glimpsed bare white skin through the thin fabric.

"Do you smoke?" She offered the box to me.

"No thanks."

She selected a cigarette, lit it with the onyx lighter that matched an oval ash tray already nearly full of butts. She took a deep drag and let the smoke drift out. "I know it's bad for me, but I just adore smoking. I bet you've never had this filthy habit?"

"I used to smoke in university but I gave it up. Cost too much."

"Smart girl." She blew one ring, and then another. "So I understand you and Aunt Margaret are good friends?"

"Not really. She comes into the store fairly often and buys a lot of books."

"Royal weddings and English country houses," Diane giggled and I joined her, smothering a twinge of disloyalty to the Pink Lady. Diane took a deep drag, and let the smoke seep out in a long steady stream from between pursed lips. "Does she talk much about me?"

I shrugged. "She talks a lot about all her family. She did say you were her favourite."

"I bet she didn't say why."

I shook my head.

Diane stared at the glowing tip of her cigarette before butting it into the nest of ashes. "She's really my mother."

"Miss Simpson?" I couldn't picture the Pink Lady pregnant, couldn't imagine her in bed with any man.

"Oh yes. She keeps her secret well hidden, don't you think?" She lit another cigarette. "I found out from Mummy years ago, one of those dreary adolescent arguments. Mummy finally said she was glad I wasn't her daughter. And that's when it all came out. Auntie Margaret got knocked up by a British war ace, if you can believe it. She and her mother went over to the Old Country to see the Coronation; she met this so charming officer and history, as they say, was made."

"Why didn't they marry?"

"The usual story. He already was. Mummy wouldn't tell me his name but assured me that he was very, very British, an honourable younger son or something."

"Doesn't sound too honourable to me."

"Well, silly old Margaret didn't even realize what was wrong with her until she was nearly five months gone. Thought the voyage home was the reason for her being sick so much. Her parents sent her to Montreal until after I was born. Geoffrey and Linda were already married and had the two boys so they agreed to take me, keep me in the family as it were."

"Does she know you know?"

"Of course not. Mummy made me promise I wouldn't tell

her. She'd be mortified. I know, though, that all this will be mine when she's gone." She waved the cigarette around the room. Ash fell on her blouse. She left it there.

"Your turn," said Simon, coming into the room. He sat down on the sofa beside me, stretching one arm out along the back; I could smell the garlic on his fingers, could feel them poised behind my shoulder. "When you've got the salad done, we can eat."

"Each to our own chore." She unfolded herself from the chair, limb by limb, stretching as she stood. She bent to stub out her cigarette. This time she caught my eye even as I looked away, embarrassed. The shawl slipped down the length of her back with the faint whisper of silk.

"Have some more wine?" she asked. "Or anything else your little heart desires?"

"Cool it, Diane," Simon snapped.

She pulled the shawl back up, tightening it over her breasts. "Just a joke," she pouted. "Maybe Rosalie likes mineral water. How am I supposed to know if I don't ask?"

"It's all right," I held up my glass. "I've still got some wine."

"I'll just go off to the kitchen then. Leave you two to catch up. So to speak."

"Don't mind her," Simon apologized. "She gets like that when she's been drinking. She says it helps to keep her mind off Jennifer. But we won't talk about that now," he added hastily, seeing the look on my face. "I want to hear all about you."

I chattered on about the move from the city and Will's business. Even when I began to list my dissatisfactions with my job, the discreet but petty politicking over the proposed manager's position, Simon listened, his head pillowed on the high rolled back of the couch, his fingers not quite touching my shoulder.

I finally stopped. "You don't want to hear about all this. You don't even know these people."

"Sometimes you just need to talk things out, hear yourself say out loud what you've been keeping to yourself. I don't mind. I kind of like it, in fact. Makes me feel that I really know you, that we really are good friends."

"Thanks," I said. I drained my glass. He filled it.

"Have you ever travelled overseas?"

I was grateful for the change of subject. "We went to Mexico for three months on Will's severance pay. It was fabulous."

"Where did you go?"

We started trading travel stories, his much more elaborate and exciting than mine. He was a practiced raconteur. My ribs soon ached from laughing. All the time I could hear Diane in the kitchen, singing along with *The Mamas and the Papas* while she rinsed lettuce and beat a dressing. She began to move in and out of the room, setting a small round table in front of the fire. The tape ended, and in the sudden silence the spit of wet wood burning and the hiss of snow on the windowpanes were the only sounds.

"More music," she shouted. "Something new, something cheerful. And let's eat."

Simon turned away from the cd player with a grin and bowed as he reached to help me stand. "*Fine Young Cannibals*," he said as the music began.

We both laughed. He kept hold of my hand. Diane was already seated, her legs tucked under the cloth, her eyes on us. I pulled slightly away. Simon hesitated before he let go.

"I hope you don't mind close quarters," Diane said. "We eat on the porch all summer. There's no dining room in here, so we cosy up to the fire and dine intimately."

Although the round table was small, it was elaborately laid with crystal, fine china and sterling cutlery. Tall white candles in brass candlesticks burned brightly.

"Oh, let's turn out the lights," Diane cried and, jumping up, she switched off all the lamps so that the room's only light came from these candles and the barred glow of the fire. A small cone of incense sent up an aromatic spiral of smoke.

"Grace." Simon's voice was so serious that it took me a moment to realize he was joking.

Diane smirked. "What's that old camp blessing? *Good food, good meat, good God, let's eat.*"

"Diane," Simon shook his head in fond reproof, and helped himself to salad.

The spaghetti was superb, its sauce a melange of thinly sliced veal, green peppers, tomatoes, olives, capers and fresh basil. The last really surprised me; the stores in our town didn't stock fresh herbs — an exotic cuisine item — in winter. Diane extolled the advantages of big city life. I wondered again why the two of them had come to the cottage out of season.

Our elbows collided as we reached for bread and cheese, our feet and legs engaged in a more intense communion under the discreet drape of Irish linen. I could not tell if the insistent pressure of Simon's knee on mine was accident, or if Diane's foot stroked my calf in mistake for his. He held my wrist to steady my hold on the heavy wooden salad bowl; she rested her hand on mine when I covered my glass to keep it from being filled once more.

"I have to drive home," I protested, laughing.

"Do you?" she said. "We have room, you can stay the night."

"No, I'll have to go, and soon. I can't believe how late it is already."

"Coffee first," Simon said. He collected a pile of plates and carried them off to the kitchen. When he snapped the switch, the sudden flood of light made me start. Diane giggled, and topped off her glass of wine. When Simon returned, he brought a tray laden with cups, a porcelain cream and sugar set, and a glass carafe of deep black coffee.

"Let's not forget the cake." It was Diane's turn to gather up the used cutlery and rush off into the other room. I half stood as if to help, but Simon shook his head.

"It's under control," he said. "You can sit and be served."

We ate the cake, a rich chocolate confection, in appreciative silence. Simon poured coffee. Diane measured three spoons of sugar into her cup and stirred it round and round. Finally, she looked at me.

"I guess it's time to talk about Jennifer," she said.

"Must we?" I asked.

"She was a very good friend," said Simon, "We both miss her dreadfully. It would help to put her to rest, so to speak, if you would tell us everything you know."

"There's not much I can tell you," I said. "I'm sorry."

I meant my touch to be one of sympathy, but he grabbed my hand in a convulsive squeeze. I looked at Diane but she didn't notice. Or pretended not to notice.

"We both loved Jennifer," she said. The tines squealed as she scraped her fork through the crumbs of cake on the rose-patterned plate. "That's why we really came out here, to be close to where it happened, see if it makes any more sense being near her. She's buried here, did you know that? Of course, you would. Did you go to the funeral?"

"I couldn't bear to."

"Oh? Why was that?"

"Finding her was so awful. I'd never seen anyone dead before, not that close up, and her back was all -- well, the gulls had been at it."

"I heard," Diane drawled the word, "that they found nothing with her at all, no clothes, no purse, no briefcase. That she was absolutely bare naked."

"She was wearing shoes."

"Shoes?" Simon's voice squeaked in surprise.

"Red shoes. No one knows why. The rest of her things were in her car. The path at the top of the dam is kind of stony. Maybe she didn't want to hurt her feet. It's weird, though. I mean, why would it matter if she was about to kill herself anyway?"

"All her things were in the car?" Diane snapped. "I thought her papers were missing. Didn't you see them anywhere lying about? Her briefcase, for instance?"

"No. I didn't stop to search around either." My voice trembled.

"We don't understand why she killed herself," Simon explained in a conciliatory tone. "We've talked it over so often ever since. She had no money problems, her law firm was doing well, she even hinted she might be getting married. In fact, we were in the middle of putting together a deal that would have been very advantageous for her. Those papers seem to be missing."

"You never met her?" Diane was insistent, leaning over the table so close to me that I could smell the coffee, wine and smoke on her breath. "Your husband never introduced you to her, or talked to you about her?"

"Why would he? He hardly knew her."

She barked a laugh. "I thought he knew her quite well."

I shook my head. "He told me they ran into each other back when he was still working in the Immigration Department. She was helping some refugees with their papers. He hasn't seen her in years."

"You believe that?" Diane ground a cigarette butt into the remains of her cake.

"Why shouldn't I?"

"They were very good friends, I thought," she said. "At least that's the way it seemed whenever we saw them together. And that was none too long ago either."

"I don't like what you're suggesting."

"I'm not suggesting anything. I just think Jennifer may have come to talk to Will about whatever was bothering her. He may have passed something along to you. Or maybe you heard she was coming and met her instead."

"I don't know what you're talking about and I don't think

you do either. I think it's time for me to go."

"Wait a minute, Rosie." Simon indicated with a quick nod of his head the empty bottle by Diane's plate. Forgive her, his expression clearly said. Forgive me.

I settled down. Diane shrugged. She felt the carafe with the back of her hand, then poured some milk into the bottom of her cup before adding the dregs of coffee.

"We had this deal going, like I told you," Simon said. "She came on one of our trips with us and after that we started to see her regularly. You know her specialty was helping refugees from Latin America. She was very good at it, really involved, not afraid to step over the line a little in the interests of her clients. I mean bribes and such. We had contacts with various government officials who could help her out and with guides and stuff when the government was not on her side. Her diary and one of the files concerning these contacts seem to be missing. They could cause trouble to quite brave people if they fell into the wrong hands. We thought perhaps she might have given them to you or Will."

"This is the second time someone has asked me the same thing."

"Who?" This time Simon clutched at my hand, his fingers digging into my palm.

I tried to pull away but he would not let go. Diane muttered a curse as coffee slopped over her saucer. She mopped at the spreading stain, then left her napkin to cover the damage. I pushed my chair back a little, freeing my feet from the confusion of legs.

"A man approached me in the park the other day, asking the same sort of questions. He seemed to think I knew all about your friend. He certainly knew a lot about me. I got scared and ran away."

"Jesus, Simon," Diane groaned. "He must be here too."

"Who?" I asked. "And how did he know that you were in the store?"

Simon opened his mouth to answer, but Diane silenced him with a slight jerk of her head. The candlelight flamed on her earrings.

"She had this friend, I guess you'd call him," she said. "He said they were engaged, but she never said anything about marrying him to us. We thought she was going with someone quite different, a man we introduced her to in Switzerland. This other guy was insanely jealous. She was terrified of him. He accused her of having affairs with everyone, even with Simon. We were in Panama when she died, but he's been phoning our house and the office, accusing Simon of murder."

"That's awful," I said. "Can't the police do anything to stop him?"

"What can they do? We had a restraining order placed on him, to keep him away from us. We thought he'd never find us out here. He's a short guy, right? Blue eyes? Balding, but still quite handsome?"

"Nothing like that. Short, yes, but with long black hair and green eyes. He was soaked to the skin when I met him. I think he'd been in the river in his suit, just below the dam where she went in."

Diane shook her head. "I don't know who that could be. Maybe he's persuaded someone else that we're to blame some-how, a friend, maybe a private detective. Did he tell you his name?"

"No."

"You almost have to pity the guy," she said. "But he's so desperate, he might be dangerous. We thought he might have killed her himself, but he was out of the country too at the time. I'll get the police to talk to him again, try to make him see that you have nothing to do with her death."

"Of course I didn't. She killed herself, didn't she?"

"It's those missing papers," Simon interrupted. "There must be some clue there as to why she did this terrible thing.

Something in her diary. You're sure she didn't give it to Will?"

"He hasn't seen or heard from her in years," I repeated.

Diane reached over and tapped my arm with one long painted finger. "Are you sure? They were close friends."

That was it. I'd had enough. I stood up, pushing my chair back into the table so hard that dishes rattled. The candle flames flickered, then steadied. "I think I'd better head home."

"We have to have those papers." Simon insisted. "It's very important."

"I don't have them. I don't know where they are." I started towards the closet where Diane had put my coat.

"You can't go yet." Her cry was both a plea and a threat.

I turned to face them. A flurry of knocks rattled the front door.

SIX

Simon was the first to move. He brushed past me, pushing me with his shoulder towards Diane. "Take her upstairs," he said. "Now."

"Come on." Diane grabbed my arm. I had no choice but to go with her up the open stairs, our feet loud on the varnished boards. The second floor extended over the back half of the house; a high railing overlooked the living room. We could hear Simon refusing someone entry, felt the rush of cold wind eddy through the hall. Diane pulled me into a room and shut the door.

"I need a smoke," she said, and sank down on the bed.

"I think you'd better tell me what's really going on," I said. She tapped a cigarette package against her palm, crumpled it, and threw it against the opposite wall. "Nothing," she muttered. She got up and went through the pockets of a jacket slung over a series of hooks that lined the wall next to the door. They were empty.

"Why did we have to come up here?"

"That's probably one of the neighbours at the door. They're so nosy about everyone who visits. Probably tattle back to Aunt Margaret about the goings on. Not that anything's going on, you know, but they have nothing better to do with their time. There's no point in all of us getting into some stupid conversation. Simon will get rid of whoever it is quickly, then we can finish our talk."

"I am finished talking. I'm ready to leave."

"Hold your horses, and sit down. It'll only take a minute." She gestured towards the bed, an antique monster whose high headboard and footboard were a tangle of wrought iron and flaking green paint.

A huge duvet fluffed and sank beneath me. I was tired and confused, tempted by the softness to lie down and go to sleep as if sleep could solve my problems. Not just the immediate question of what the Harpers were up to, but everything that rolled and tumbled around my head: Will and his work, my empty womb, my pointless job.

Diane crossed the room to an armoire whose yellow mirror cast her figure in a warped and wavering shade. From a cloth bag strung to the door knob, she dug out a leather pouch. She took the hand mirror from the dresser and, sitting down cross-legged on the floor, proceeded to pour a small amount of white powder on the glass. She divided this into four lines with a razor blade, chopping and scraping them into equal portions.

"What are you doing?" I demanded.

She looked up through the curls that bunched on her forehead. "Don't you ever watch TV? This is coke. Grade A."

She picked up a short glass straw, bent over the mirror and snorted deeply, indelicately. One line disappeared, then the second. She tossed her head back and pinched her nose. For a moment she held the pose stiffly at attention. Then, her whole body relaxed, a doll deflating. She opened her eyes and smiled at me, holding out the tray with the remaining lines.

"No thanks." I drew back.

She shrugged. "More for me."

She sniffed up the other two lines, then wetted her index finger and wiped the residue up. Baring her lips, she rubbed her gums, smacking her teeth. "Let it snow, let it snow, let it snow," she giggled.

"I know she's up there." A male voice, loud with anger, echoed up the stairs.

Diane shifted position so that she knelt between the door and the bed.

"What do you all want with me?" I asked again. "Why won't you believe me when I say I know nothing about any papers, any meetings? I found her body and that's it. Nothing more. Why are we hiding up here? Why don't we just go down and tell that man to leave us all alone?"

"Won't work," Diane muttered. "He won't believe you."

"Why not? And what about you. What do you believe?"

"I believe you're in over your head, that's for sure," she giggled again and combed her fingers up through her hair. "Why don't you just relax?"

"I want to go home."

"You can't always get what you want," she hummed. "But need, now, there's a different story."

Lifting her arms, and swaying as if to music, she pulled off the red shirt. She cupped one breast as if weighing it, traced the blue vein from her neckbone down over its soft swell to tease the nipple further. Her tongue peeked between her teeth.

"Cut it out, Diane."

She ignored me. Her fingers continued, counting down her ribs, sliding over the tautness of her belly, a hollow between the sharp blades of her pelvic bones. She stretched her legs apart.

I stood up. "That's enough."

The front door slammed, but she didn't look up. I tried to edge around her. She grabbed my ankle.

"Aren't you a little hot in here?" she purred. "Why don't you make yourself more comfortable?"

"For Christ's sake, Diane," Simon said, pushing open the door. It struck her back and she winced. Her hands flew to cover her breasts, and she gasped back a tiny sob.

Simon's face was flushed a mottled red that highlighted a nest of wrinkles around his eyes that I had not noticed before. "Get dressed," he hissed. And to me, "I'm sorry about this."

"I thought we might forget about business for awhile. Let's party." She sniffed, rubbed her nose with the back of one hand.

"I'm leaving," I repeated.

Simon sighed, but stood away, opening the door. I forced myself to walk slowly down the stairs, to find my coat and check that I had my keys. I couldn't make out the words, but I could hear Simon's voice hurried in argument and Diane's low laughter in reply. I was bent over pulling on my boots when he came down the stairs. He raised one hand as if to touch me but let it drop.

"Good-bye," I said.

"You can't just go like this," he answered. "I'm sorry about Diane. Sometimes she gets a little crazy. She doesn't cope with stress well."

"That's what you call it? Stress? I thought she was supposed to be so upset about her friend's death."

"She is. She has a problem with drugs. I guess you saw. I didn't think she had anything with her, she promised she'd stay clean while we were here, until this trouble over Jennifer's papers got cleared up."

"I don't understand," I said, "Why do you think I have these papers? If I'd found anything like that I would have given them to the police."

"No," he nearly shouted.

I recoiled.

He passed one hand over his face and spoke in a voice that was trying hard to sound reasonable. "Don't do that. Jennifer could be very unwise in what she wrote down. I know there are things in the diary that shouldn't be made public."

"Like what?"

"Stuff about Diane."

"So all this is about protecting your wife?"

He shrugged. "You will give her papers to me?"

"Simon, I don't have them. I've never seen them. Will doesn't know anything about them either. He would have told me if he'd met her again, if she had given him anything."

"Charming to see such faith."

I felt the skin across my cheeks tighten and burn.

"You're blushing," Simon laughed.

I stood up. With shoes and purse in one fist, I grabbed the door knob with the other. Simon put both hands flat against it, holding it shut and me imprisoned.

"Let me go," I said. I refused to turn around, to face him.

"What I don't understand," he said, "is why you still care about him, why you're protecting him."

"What do you mean?"

"Come on, Rosie! Are you trying to tell me that, in what, fifteen years of marriage, Will has never been with another woman? I knew Jennifer very well; if she wanted to sleep with him, she'd sleep with him."

"Will doesn't lie to me."

"So tell me why she came to see him when she was in trouble?"

"How do you know it was him she came to see?"

"She didn't know anyone else in this town."

"She was born here, she must have relatives, family friends."

"Jennifer wasn't the type to keep up with family."

"Well there you go. Will hadn't seen her in at least five years. She'd have no reason to come looking for him."

"She'd heard from him recently. She told us."

"I don't believe you."

"Rosie, Rosie," Simon shook his head. "You've always been such a romantic."

"Enough," I said. "Let me go."

Simon didn't move. "You'd better think this through. I don't want to see you hurt."

"Is that a threat?"

When I turned he caught me by the shoulders, pressed his mouth hard on mine. His left hand gripped my head, forcing it back; his right slipped inside my coat to pull at my sweater. I struggled, stamping on his feet and elbowing his chest to escape the pressure of his body. I got one elbow under his chin; the other dug into his diaphragm. At last I pried him off me.

We stared at each other, our breathing loud and grated.

"You liked it," he said.

I opened the door.

"You know you liked it," he repeated. "I want you to stay."

"Leave me alone," I spat. I stepped outside and drew a deep breath. The clean air seared my nostrils, my lungs. "I don't want to see you ever again. Or your wife. If you come near me or even phone me, I'll call the police. I'll have you arrested for attempted rape."

"Rosie," he pleaded.

But I was on the porch now. Free. I stalked out to the car. I would have liked to slam the door and drive off in a squeal of gravel, but instead had to warm up the engine and scrape the ice and snow from the windows. I wouldn't look back but I knew Simon was watching me. I think he called my name once more as I got into the car and buckled the seatbelt. I didn't pay any attention.

A sudden darkness came with the closing of the front door. I rested my head on the wheel for just a moment, taking slow deep breaths to calm the beating of my heart. My hands and feet of their own volition took control of the gearshift, the gas pedal. As the car circled the drive, the headlights swept across the housefront. Through the uncurtained window, I could see Simon talking into the telephone. Diane, still nude and smoking one of her cigarettes, was weaving down the stairs.

The snow was thick on the lane, still drifting lazily down though a full moon now brightened the sky with an eerie silver light that flashed off and on as clouds bunched and scurried across it. Footsteps between the ruts my car had made earlier in the evening disappeared at the roadside. A plow had gone by and for a moment I feared I would get stuck in the small drift thrown up across the drive. I gunned through, righted the skid, and drove carefully over the sanded ice of the dirt road to the highway. It was bare, but the wind swept clouds of snow across from the fields, so that for moments visibility was reduced to a few feet. Luckily there was no traffic coming towards me so I could use the high beams to illuminate the ditches.

The highway was narrow and wound in looping curves along the river bank where the water still flowed black and frothing over the rocks towards the hydro dams that were flung across it every few miles. On the other side fields alternated with woodlots, the lights of an occasional farmhouse glimmering far down drifted lanes. I passed the town limit sign, and smiled. The council had elected to extend the boundaries far beyond current building in the hope of gaining tax dollars when, eventually, development would swallow the river front. So far, nothing had been built and the only difference between county and municipality was the simple white sign and a lot of hope.

I began to relax and to get angry. I hoped the missing papers would surface in a tabloid. I hoped that scandal would drive the Harpers out of the country, out of my life forever. Lights crept up behind me and I swerved back into my own lane, easing up on the gas. I hadn't drunk much, but enough that I had to concentrate on the driving.

The headlights in the rearview mirror crept closer. I realized they had been there since I turned off the cottage road on to the highway. I dimmed my lights, but the other driver did the opposite so that my car was filled with brightness, blinding the road ahead. I cursed, beeped my horn in protest, drove faster. The other car began to gain on me. Desperate to escape the lights, I pulled over into the next lane. He followed me there too. Back I went to my own side of the road, the wheels threatening a skid. I scraped on to the shoulder, too close to the water for comfort.

A car passed in the other direction, slowed, kept going.

Now the following car was beside me. I braked to let him pass. He simply kept pace. I risked a quick glance to my left; the interior light switched on and the man from the park smirked at me, his mouth moving as he talked into a cellular phone. His car made a sudden swerve towards my rear fender. I wrestled with the wheel as the Honda went into a spin.

By luck, I kept the car on the road, faced in the right direction. I pulled over on to the narrow shoulder, only inches away from the dark rushing water, switched off the motor, and released my breath in a long sigh that trailed into a whimper. I managed to open the window, hoping that the shock of air would clear my head, and steady the staccato tattoo of my pulse.

That's when I realized that the other car had also stopped, some few yards in front. The door opened and the man got out, his hand gripping some sort of club. It was too late to turn my car around, to head back to the dubious safety of Simon's house. I turned my beams on full and began to back up.

Another set of lights appeared in the rearview mirror, this time red as well as white. The still night was split by the whooping of a siren. The man stopped, then jumped back into his car and took off. A spotlight glared on the scene: the black strip of highway and running water, the white of the snowbanks, the lazy falling flakes.

My gloved fingers fumbled at the knob of the door lock. By the time I had the door opened, my breath had barely steadied. I slipped out of the car, grabbed the door frame with one hand, but was on my knees when the policeman reached me. He stood for a minute, then stuck out his hand to haul me up. Almost as broad as he was tall and made more solid by the weight of his fur-lined leather jacket and the equipment slung from his belt, he stared down at me as though ticking off my appearance on a list.

"Constable Olan, city force, ma'am," he said. "What's the trouble?"

I clung to his arm, pointed up the road. The other car had

disappeared. "There was someone chasing me," I said.

He glanced up the road, then stared at me. His eyes were a very pale blue under the peak of his cap, the stubble of his beard white on the ruddy glow of his cheeks. He hardly bothered to check a yawn.

"I didn't see any other car," he said. "You were all over the road back there, going too fast."

"He forced me to stop," I insisted. "He almost drove me into the river."

"This guy got a name?"

I shook my head, sniffed back the tears.

"Have you been drinking?"

"No," I shouted. "Well, not much, just some wine at dinner."

"Got your licence, registration?"

"You don't believe me." I dropped his arm and hugged myself. The wind billowed my skirt, slid icy hands up my legs. I needed desperately to go to the bathroom.

"About the drinking? We can soon settle that."

"I mean about that man I was trying to get away from. He was out of his car, coming after me with some kind of weapon when you turned up."

"What's the trouble, Frank?" A second cop materialized on the other side of the Honda. In spite of the cold he was bareheaded, his thin red hair gelled perfectly in even waves, a curl kissing his forehead. One hand picked at his moustache, the other rested on the pommel of his gun.

"Lady here says some guy was after her," Olan reported.

"Oh yeah?" The younger man looked me up and down. "Been out on the town tonight, eh lady? Heading home kind of early, aren't you? Bars don't close for another hour at least."

"I was at a dinner party," I said. "I'm not drunk, I'm not crazy. That man was going to hurt me and all you do is stand here and treat me as if I've done something wrong."

"Didn't like the company, eh? Some guy coming on a little too strong? Thought you needed some fresh air?"

"Can it, Paulie," the older man said. He turned to me. "We saw your car couldn't seem to keep on the right side of the road. We didn't notice anyone else. Now why don't you hand me your wallet, let me take a look. Constable Leary has a little box with him there. You just take a deep breath and blow in it real slow, okay?"

"No." I sat down on the car seat, my feet still on the ground. I sniffled, took off my glasses to wipe tears away with the back of my hand. "If you look, you'll see the tire marks in the snow where he stopped his car. You'll see his footprints too. He was coming after me, I tell you."

Olan peered along the path of my headlights. The ruts and prints were already half-filled with snow. He walked forward, stepping with caution on the slick of black ice that covered the tarmac. His partner and I both watched him.

"Look, lady," Leary said. "We don't much like standing around here in the storm. Let's get the formalities over with and we can all go home."

I shook my head. "I'm not drunk. There's nothing wrong with me."

Olan kicked a small drift of snow which powdered over his pant leg. A plow roared by in the other direction, its blue light flashing, sand spraying behind it. In its wake, a long dark car slowed as it passed. I thought I recognized its shape but there were two people in it this time, both staring our way. Olan came back.

"Okay," he said. "There's marks there all right. Just like you said."

"Jesus, Frank," Leary complained.

Olan ignored him. He flipped open a notebook, hunching over to protect the pages from the snow. "You see the guy? Know who he was? Can you give us a description?"

"I think it was a man I saw near my house last week," I said.

Leary muttered something under his breath and stomped back to his car. The door slammed. Olan sighed, "You don't know for sure though?"

"When he passed me, I thought it was him." I described the man in the park. "And I think he came to the house where I was having dinner. Simon and Diane Harper's. They're staying up at the lake in the Simpson cottage."

"Frank!" Leary called. "Let's get a move on."

Olan looked back. "Sorry about him," he said. "His wife just up and left. He's not feeling too good about anyone these days."

"That's all right," I tried to curb my anger. "Can you find this guy?"

"We'll look around. What kind of car was it?"

"Big and black. I didn't get the licence plate either."

He shut the book. "Drive carefully now," he said. "We'll follow you home, make sure you get there safely."

I pulled my legs inside. My feet were freezing. The engine coughed twice before it caught and the Honda lurched out on to the road. I drove at a steady 60 kph, both hands on the wheel. I sang all the verses to all the songs I could remember, mostly carols that rang with childhood peace and expectancy. No other cars passed. The headlights stayed in my rearview mirror all the way home.

SEVEN

"What happened?" Will looked from me to the police car parked at the curb. "Are you all right, Rosie?"

"You're Mr. Cairns?" Olan joined me on the porch. The wind rattled the screen door which Will held open, blocking Sadie's welcome with his body. "Your wife had some trouble. Driving in weather like this, late at night and alone."

"Someone tried to drive me off the road," I said.

"She thinks someone's after her," Olan continued as if I hadn't spoken. "You know anything about it?"

Will wouldn't look at me. "You remember that Rumble drowning?" When Olan nodded, he continued, "Rosie found the body. And since then, she's been nervous."

"Will!" I was outraged.

"It's true, Rosie. I've been talking to Karen and she agrees you've been acting strange, not yourself." He turned back to the cop. "Constable Finlay was here the other day. He knows all about it."

"Okay." Olan shook his head at me. "Well, you're home safe now. You've been talking to Finlay, have you? You should have told me before. You think of anything else, or notice anything else out of place, you contact me or him, you hear?"

"Right," I muttered. "So everyone will think I'm crazy."

Both men pretended they hadn't heard. Olan shook Will's hand, and patted my arm. "Goodnight then," he said. "You be careful now, Mrs. Cairns." He trudged back down the path.

"How could you say that about me?" I demanded.

Will stepped back into the house. "Come out of the snow," he urged.

I didn't move. "You think I'm making all this up."

"Sadie will get loose," he said. "And you're letting out the heat."

I came in and he hugged me. I stood still, watching dark spots spread on the rug as my coat dripped in the sudden warmth of the hall.

"Don't be mad at me, Rosie," he said. "I'm worried about you."

"You've got a funny way of showing it, implying that I'm round the bend."

"Take off your coat and come and sit down and tell me what happened. I'll get you a drink."

"Stop humouring me," I yelled.

Sadie whined and thrust her head hard against my hand.

"All right." Will sat on the stairs. "What happened?"

"A car followed me from Simon's house, then tried to force me into the river. I'm sure it was that man I saw in the park, I could see him talking into a phone. And before I left the house, I saw Simon on the phone too. And I'm sure it was him who came to the house but Diane took me upstairs so I wouldn't meet him."

"Slow down." Will grabbed my hands to still them.

"I was terrified. The car swerved and I thought I was going in the river for sure. And then he got out of his car with some kind of weapon. It looked like a bat. He was going to hurt me, Will, I know he was. And I don't know why."

"What did the cops do?"

"He took off when he heard the siren. I don't think they saw him or believed me. You didn't help much."

"It's hard to see how you could recognize someone in the dark."

"He turned the light on inside his car. I think he wanted me to know it was him."

"Why?"

"I don't know why." This time I couldn't keep the tears back. Will handed me a tissue. "I think we'd better speak to Finlay again."

"What's the use?" I wiped my face. "All you men have decided I'm having some kind of breakdown."

"That's not true, Rosie. We're just worried about you."

I blew my nose. "I want to go to bed, and forget about it." I hung my coat on the hook, pulled my boots off and lined them up on the tray by the heater vent.

"I can't stand to see you like this," Will said. "Let's go back out to the lake and talk to your friend Simon. Find out who this man is who you say has been bothering you."

"No."

He looked at me, surprised. "I thought you wanted to get this mystery solved. If the guy came to the cottage, then obviously Harper knows who he is, so he can get him to leave you alone."

"I can't go back there."

"Why not?"

"The Harpers are just too far out for me. I don't want to see them again."

"You can't just leave it like that. You have to tell me what happened tonight."

I put my hand on his arm. "It doesn't matter. It's over. Let's just go to bed and get some sleep."

"Did they hurt you?"

"No, it was nothing like that, nothing I couldn't handle. But very unpleasant."

"What? You can't just leave me wondering."

"It was crazy, Will. We had a perfectly ordinary dinner until they started asking questions about Jennifer Rumble. They both said you were having an affair with her."

Will rubbed his chin. "You didn't believe that, did you?"

He stared at my hands which were squeezed together. He could see the white knuckles, but couldn't feel the crescents of pain I dug into my palms to keep myself awake, alert, aware of every word he said. And everything he didn't say.

I didn't answer that question but continued with my story. "Diane took me up to their bedroom when someone knocked on the door. We could hear Simon arguing with another man. I don't know who, but I can guess. Diane was in a strange mood all night. Maybe she was trying to distract me from what was going on downstairs. Anyway she got out some cocaine and started to strip off all her clothes. I tried to stop her, but she was too high. Simon came in and yelled at her. Then he tried to force me to stay."

"Oh, Rosie. I should have gone with you."

"They think I know some big secret. They think you know it too."

"What secrets? Those papers? There weren't any papers, were there?"

"Not you, too!"

"Don't listen to me. I'm upset, I don't know what I'm saying." He sighed.

"Nothing makes sense," I agreed. "You wouldn't believe how strangely they both behaved. I felt trapped in a movie. Maybe they thought if I wouldn't give them what they want on my own, they could seduce me into helping them. Only it felt more like rape."

"I'm calling Finlay." Will turned towards the kitchen.

I grabbed his arm. "Let it rest, Will. Nothing happened. If the cops go out there, they'll both be outraged and Diane will put on her lady-of-the-manor act — if she's straight enough. They'll deny anyone came to the door and say that I ran away for no reason. I know they'll lie. They're good at it. But they won't bother me again. I made it pretty clear that I want nothing to do with them any more. And they must believe now that I don't know anything about any papers."

"If you won't let me call the police, then you must come out to their place with me tomorrow."

I shook my head. "I can't go back there."

"You'll have to, Rosie, just once more. We'll be together in daylight. They won't hurt you if I'm there too. We'll get this thing straightened out once and for all."

"They think you had something to do with Jennifer Rumble's death," I said. "They said you met her not very long ago."

"Then obviously they're lying. Finlay was just here. I went through the whole thing with him, my 'relationship' with her, such as it was. He's checked it out. If there was anything to it, don't you think he'd be back here by now with more questions?"

"I don't know what to think any more," I sighed.

For long moments we stared at each other. Will dropped his eyes first. "It's too late for all this now. We'll talk in the morning."

I woke to an empty bed and the sound of rain pelting the windows, the plop of water dripping into a bucket. Downstairs, water trickled from a stain spreading over the back porch door. It had formed a puddle which Will had briefly mopped, then left covered with newspapers that were already soaked through. By the time he got back with Sadie from her morning walk, I had cleaned up the water and placed two more pots under the worse drips.

"We'll have to have the roof fixed," I said as soon as he came in. He shook his head and threw the morning paper on the table. Sadie tracked mud over the floor, heading toward her favourite spot on the hall rug. He caught her.

"What a mess," he said. "I'll take her downstairs and wash her off. I might need some help."

"I'll start the coffee."

He didn't call me, though I heard his curses and the dog's whines as he struggled with her to wash the slush off her legs and pull the salt out of her paws. She hated baths. I heard him howl as she soaked him with one vigorous shake, her favourite trick. I took my mug and the paper into the living room as he went upstairs to change into dry clothes.

"I guess we should get a move on if we're going to go up to the lake today," Will said a while later.

I put down the travel section. He sat hunched in the rocking chair, newspaper in a semicircle on the floor around him.

"What's the use? They won't tell us anything."

"I'll make them prove that they're lying about Jennifer Rumble and me."

"You don't have to prove anything," I said. "I know you. If you say you hadn't seen her in years, then I believe you. I've always trusted you, you know that."

"What about the man in the car?"

"Maybe I was imagining things. It was late and I was upset because of what had happened, Simon and Diane and the dope and all. It was so weird out there."

"If we go together . . ."

I shook my head. "Besides, it's still raining."

"Are you sure? I'm more than happy to have it out with them."

"No. Sleeping dogs are better left alone."

"Let's go to bed."

"You're tired?"

He smiled. "Sleep's not what I had in mind."

"I don't know. I'm not feeling terrific."

He came to kneel by the couch where I lay stretched out under an afghan blanket knitted years ago by his mother. Neither of us spoke. He stroked my face lightly with one finger, tracing the line of brow, cheekbone, nose, lips. I put my arms around him, relishing the solid width of his shoulders, surprised by the faint trembling that pulsed through his skin.

The phone rang. I tried to pull away, but Will held me close, his eyes still closed, his mouth on mine. Six rings. He let me go.

"Do you want to answer?" he asked.

"No. Let's go upstairs."

The phone stopped after the twelfth ring. We were already undressed and under the duvet when it began again. Will groaned and flopped over on his back.

"It must be important." I said. "I'll answer it."

It was cold in the study, the sleet rattling against the window. I picked up the phone, staring out through the window at the street where a car was parked, its lights off and a small plume of smoke rising from the muffler. I couldn't see who was in it. It didn't look big enough to be the car that had chased me last night. I pulled down the blind. My lower back ached and as I spoke, I massaged it with my free hand.

"Where have you been?" It was Karen. "I've been trying to reach you."

"Walking Sadie," I lied.

"On a day like this? You guys are martyrs. Listen, I had to call you. Dunstable came into the store yesterday asking all sorts of questions about you."

"What sort of questions?"

"Your husband's name, what he does for a living, where you live, your phone number."

"Did you tell him anything?"

"I didn't, but Stephanie was there. He came in just as we were changing shifts. She gave him your number."

"Why would she do that?"

"He said it was urgent that he speak to you."

"That's all I need, to have him and his Bible-thumpers come knocking on my door."

"I think it's more than that, Rosie. He seemed very upset about something. I told him you'd be back in the store on Monday, but he said he had to see you as soon as possible. Have you heard from him?"

"No. But neither of us was home last night."

"Will went to dinner at the Harper's after all?" Karen couldn't disguise her surprise.

"I went alone. He had to go into the shop. Neither of us got home till quite late."

"So how did it go?"

"Look, this isn't a good time to talk. I'll call you later, okay?"

"Okay. Oh, wait a minute," she shouted as I was about to hang up. "There's something else. Dunstable was about to give a message to me for you when another man came in the store. As soon as the Reverend saw him, he shut right up and left."

"What did the other guy look like?"

"I wasn't paying much attention. I was glad to see Dunstable go, and the other man left right away as well. Miss Simpson was there, nattering away about Diane, Stephanie was going on about the manager job again, and I just wanted to get home." She paused. "Are you all right? Is there something going on I should know about?"

"I'll talk to you later. It was probably coincidence."

"I saw Dunstable and the other man out on the street. They seemed to be arguing. I thought I should tell you."

"Yes, thanks, it was good of you to call. But I really must go." I went back in the bedroom.

Will was sitting up, glasses on. He put down a book.

"That was Karen. Apparently Dunstable came into the store yesterday looking for me. I wonder what he wants?"

"I know what I want." Will lifted the duvet, inviting me in.

I came back to our bed.

EIGHT

The doorbell's chime set Sadie barking. I rolled over away from
Will who yawned and stretched, his feet seeking out mine under
the tangle of sheets. Gray light filled the room with shadows.

"Let's pretend we're not here," I said. Our visitor began
banging on the glass fanlight. Sadie's yelps rose higher.

"I'd better get it before the dog strangles herself," Will said.
"You sleep longer if you want." He vaulted out of bed, pulled his
track pants from the pile of clothes on the floor, and a shirt from
the closet. He yelled at Sadie to be quiet as he ran downstairs. I
lay snuggled deep in the warmth we had made. Sadie's bark
subsided to a growl as the door clicked open.

"Good afternoon. You must be Mr. Cairns." I recognized
Dunstable's voice.

"Yes." Will's answer was curt.

"I wonder if I might have a word with your wife. I believe
she's at home?"

I started to dress.

"She's not available right now. Perhaps you could leave a
message with me?"

"No, I must speak with her." His voice cracked.

I came slowly down the stairs. The Reverend perched on
the doorstep, one foot on the sill to keep it open. He was used to
unwelcoming householders. Every year his church urged its
members to proselytize in their neighbourhoods. We'd had our
share of soberly suited men, clutching open Bibles, urging us to

repent and be saved. But Dunstable was empty-handed.

"Don't let him in," I said to Will.

He looked up at me, surprised, but didn't move from his post blocking the door. Sadie bared her teeth in a grin that frightened the Reverend. He stepped back out on the porch, glancing over his shoulder up and down the street. The wind drove freezing rain across the lawns into the white mist that shrouded the park.

"What do you want?" I asked.

"I just want to talk to you for a few minutes." Dunstable raised one hand as if in blessing. "I don't mean any harm, you must believe me. Please, may I come in?"

"All right. You can have five minutes."

Will stood back only far enough to let the Reverend close the door behind him. I stayed on the stairs, ready to retreat to the study where there was a lock on the door, a telephone. Will ordered Sadie to sit, but kept his hand on her collar.

Dunstable rubbed his hands together. "I don't quite know how to begin," he said. "It's a difficult story." He looked into the living room but neither of us moved. "It's about Miss Rumble, Jennifer Rumble."

"Not you too." I sat down on the steps, suddenly tired.

"She had some business with us, with my church." Dunstable kept his eyes on the floor, as if the pattern in the old hall runner fascinated him, the intricate interweaving of peacocks and flowers in faded reds and greens. Sadie thumped her tail, willing to be friends. We all ignored her. "It seems there are some papers missing. I wondered if she gave them to you?"

"For the thousandth time, no. She was dead when I found her. I never saw her before then. I never spoke to her."

"And you?" Dunstable turned to Will.

"No." His fists balled.

"Ah well, I just thought I should ask." Dunstable ducked his head. One vein pulsed blue under thin strands of graying hair combed in neat lines across his skull. "I'll not disturb you any longer." He reached behind him for the doorknob.

Will caught hold of his sleeve. The man's hand dangled from his wrist nerveless, bone white.

"Tell us what the mystery is."

"There is no mystery, not really. It's just that she had some personal matters mixed in with her business files, matters personal to me and the church."

"I don't recall any mention of a connection between her and your church," I said. "I thought part of the puzzle about her suicide is why she chose to come here to die."

Dunstable shook his head so fiercely that one thread of hair broke loose from its oily anchor and flopped down over his eyes. He combed it back in place with fingers that shook with more than cold. "That had nothing to do with us, nothing at all. We are of course sorry that such a fine young woman should be in such despair, that we could not offer her any comfort. The police are quite satisfied that our business with her was not relevant." He pulled his arm away from Will and pushed the door wide open. The wind blew a splatter of rain across the porch.

"Hold on a minute," I demanded. "Will, shut the door before we all freeze. Thanks. Now, tell me who's been following me. Is it someone from your church, someone you know?"

Dunstable quivered, his back still to me. "I don't know what you're talking about."

"The man who met you in the bookstore yesterday."

"That was something quite unrelated."

"Everything's unrelated, according to you. My friend told me she saw you arguing with him, and this just after you were asking all sorts of questions about me."

Dunstable's head twitched again, as if shaking off a bothersome fly. Will and I waited, but he refused to speak, just stood there with his head bent, his hand on the doorknob. A car horn hooted outside. We all three jumped.

"I must go," Dunstable whispered. "I apclogize for disturbing you."

"There's another thing," I said. "Simon Harper says the
missing papers are a diary and a refugee claimant file. Nothing
to do with any church."

"Simon Harper?" Dunstable jerked around to face me.
"You know him?"

"He was in the store the other day. Don't you remember?"

"That was him? I didn't realize . . . But how do you know
him?" His teeth worried at his lower lip. "What's he up to?" He
wasn't asking us but talking to himself.

"We just want to know what's going on," Will said. "Rosie
has been threatened twice and now you come around asking
questions as well. Why don't you come in and sit down. I'll call
Constable Finlay, see if he can come over, and help make sense
of all this."

"No, no police." Dunstable clutched Will's elbow. "There's
no need to bring the police into this. I talked with them already."
He paused, sighed, and continued. "Miss Rumble could be quite
inconsiderate with her assessment of people and situations. She
had a tendency to embroider facts a little, to exaggerate, to put
herself in a dramatic role. I'm worried about what she may have
said about the church, some of its younger members, in her diary.
The church, as you know, is under attack these days, some of our
more flamboyant brethren have made mistakes that reflect badly
on all of us. She may have implied things that aren't true, that
might cause considerable harm."

"What kinds of things?" I asked.

He waved one arm in the air. "Oh, anything at all that's
likely to cause distress. I do not like to speak ill of any person, but
she was not very kind."

"She had something on you?" I persisted .

He straightened, suddenly ramrod stiff. "Of course not. Just
nastiness, rumours, gossip. That sort of thing."

"You'd think, then," said Will, "that she'd leave the diary somewhere to be found. If she wanted to cause trouble, that is."

Dunstable shook his head. "Who knows what the poor creature may have done or felt in her despair? Perhaps she thought better of her ways in the end and destroyed it herself." He opened the door and quickly stepped through. "I must be going. Good day."

He stumbled down the steps, grabbing cedar branches for support. A black Ford sedan idled at the curb. The driver, a boy with close-cropped hair, leaned over to open the door, then gunned away as soon as Dunstable was seated.

"I'm going to call Finlay," Will said.

"It's Sunday," I pointed out. "He may not be in."

"Worth a try. We should tell him about this visit right away. Maybe suggest he talk to Dunstable again."

"You think the Reverend has something to do with Rumble's death?"

"He seems pretty worried about something. Whatever he's hiding, I'm sure it concerns that creep who's been after you. Maybe the cops need to look into this church connection a bit more closely. He certainly seems to have had a lot more to do lately with Jennifer than I've had."

"But the police don't suspect you of anything. Do they?"

"Of course not. I told them everything I knew about her. Which isn't much." Will headed for the kitchen phone. "It just wouldn't hurt to hand them a clue when it falls in our laps like this."

Finlay wasn't in. Will left a message for him. "He'll probably call tomorrow."

"I'm working."

"Me too. Well, he has my shop number, he knows you're at the store."

I still sat on the stairs. Will rested his hand on the bannister railing. His fingernails were bitten to the skin. "I guess I should get back to work?" He raised his eyebrows, cocked his head toward the bedroom door.

I yawned. "I think I'll have a bath."

"Right." Will's hand dropped and he turned towards the living room where a file of plans lay open on the coffee table.

"I've been thinking about what you said last night," I said. I'll call Simon and see if he's willing to talk to the two of us together. Maybe we can get to the root of all this nonsense, and get it over with."

"Good idea."

No one answered, though I let the phone ring a dozen times. That evening, almost every hour on the hour, I kept calling. The next two tries, the line was busy. My third call was answered by a distant electronic voice which informed me that the line had been disconnected.

"Wires must be down," Will said. "We'll go out tomorrow afternoon if the storm's over."

All night the blizzard raged, the wind rushing winter down from the north. When I struggled out of my dream — the familiar nightmare chase by uniformed Nazis through a foreign blacked-out landscape, my speed impeded by the scarlet spiked heels welded to my feet — pale light silvered the frost flowers on the window.

There must have been a power failure; the digital clock pulsed with a flat signal, the alarm silenced. I shook Will awake and we stumbled through the cold house and a hasty breakfast, both of us late for work.

The snow lay thick on the ground, our street, as usual, left unplowed until busier thoroughfares were dealt with. I shovelled the driveway while Will warmed up the car. It wasn't until he left and I started to walk down to the bus stop that I noticed the pattern etched into the front lawn — a stick hangman, the letter R.

I went back indoors and called Finlay. He still wasn't there. I stood for a long minute with one hand on the phone, staring out the window. A giant blue spruce obscured the facade of the house across the street. While I watched, a great lump of snow slid down its skirt, from branch to branch, to a white and silent explosion on the ground. I pulled my mitts back on and went off to catch the bus.

It was a normal Monday morning in the store. I vacuumed the rug and straightened the books, filled out a couple of order sheets. The only customer departed without buying anything. No one called. I phoned Will once to tell him about the sign in the snow and to ask if he'd heard from Finlay.

He hadn't. "I'll pick you up at noon," he said. "We'll go straight out to see the Harpers whether we've heard from Finlay by then or not."

I tried calling Simon as well, but his line was still out of order. I was too restless to read, so I finally resorted to cleaning the shelves in the mystery section, piling the books row by row on the floor and washing down the varnished boards, dusting spines and jackets before replacing them. It was a mindless job, but it filled the time before Lil arrived for her shift.

"Hello, hello," she carolled, entering the store in a blast of icy air. "Isn't it beautiful outside? Real Christmassy weather."

"Close the door, it's freezing."

"My, you look busy." She opened the door to the basement where a couple of hooks served as an excuse for a cupboard. She deposited her boots on a plastic bag she had spread on the floor, and slipped on a pair of loafers she kept there. After combing her hair, she touched up her lipstick before coming back into the room.

"There've been no customers all morning," I told her as she went to check the till.

She played her fingers absently over the cash register keys. "I guess you've heard all about Dr. Long's plans for the store?" she asked.

"It's a good idea," I said. "She certainly doesn't care much about it. So are you all set to be the new manager?"

"Oh, I couldn't," she gasped. "There's so much involved. Fred wouldn't like it."

"Have you talked to him about it?"

"No. Not yet."

"I think he'd be proud of you."

"I can't very well say anything until I know for sure. I mean, if I tell him I might have the job and then Dr. Long gives it to someone else, he'll insist I leave. I like working here, I don't want to have to quit."

"If you want to be manager, I can't see why you couldn't be. You know the store better than any of the rest of us, you've worked here longest. You know all the sales reps, all the school librarians, all the special customers."

"Stephanie thinks it might be too much for me," Lil said.

"Oh Stephanie." I threw the sponge into the pail. A small wave slopped over the side on to the gray carpet. I rubbed at it with the dust cloth. "Don't you worry about Stephanie. She won't stand in your way if Karen and I both say that we think you should take over."

"Maybe she's right."

"Maybe you should start thinking about what you want. You've run the store for as long as I've known you with Dr. Long constantly at your shoulder. Just think how much more fun it'll be to work without her nosing around all the time. You could start those after school readings you were talking about. Invite some children's authors in and get the teachers involved."

"Do you think I could?"

"I don't see why not. It would certainly bring in more customers." I looked around the empty room. "The store certainly needs something."

"Are you coming to the meeting after work today?"

"What meeting?"

"With Dr. Long. Stephanie arranged it."

"She conveniently forgot to tell me about it." I picked up the pail. "I have to go out this afternoon. If I'm done in time, I'll be back. But Karen will be here, I assume. She knows how I feel."

The sink and a barely functioning toilet were in a closet in the basement. I put the cleaning stuff away and picked out an armload of books to take back upstairs.

"Merry Christmas," I heard Lil's cheery greeting.

The answer was a barely audible grunt, a rising inflection. "Rosie's here?"

"She's downstairs." Lil's answer was short and offended.

"Did Finlay ever phone?" Will called down to me.

"No." I put the books down on the landing and pulled on my coat and mitts.

"Isn't that the detective you talked to when you found that poor woman's body?" Lil followed us to the door. "Has something else happened?"

"No," I lied, "just some routine matters. But if he calls, will you ask him to come by our house tonight? We'll be home by six, at the latest."

"Don't forget the meeting."

"Right. I'll try to get back here first."

I described the drawing in the snow to Will once we were in the car and on our way.

"Those kids again," he growled. "Probably the ones who put that little fire on our porch. You must have really made them mad."

"So everything's my fault?" I punched at the thermostat, trying to force more warmth out of the heater.

Will didn't answer.

We listened to the radio on the drive out to Mud Lake. A retired hockey player recalled some winning goals and the commentator commiserated with him about the dismal state of the game since Gretzky went Hollywood. It's always been difficult for me to understand why grown men can care so passionately for a sport corrupted by advertising and big business. I would have turned it off, but their conversation at least alleviated the necessity for talk between us.

The road down to the lake had recently been plowed and our tires crunched over the sand and salt. We smelled smoke before we reached the Simpson cottage, and spotted a patrol car parked there before we could see what was left of the house: the smouldering roof collapsed inside a skeleton of blackened uprights, the chimney pipe twisted, still rising from a melted iron lump that stuck upright, a thumb poking through blistered shingles. The snow had been trampled into sooty ruts and icicles sheathed the trees. A young cop got out of the car and waved us on. Will rolled down the window.

"What happened here?"

The cop slapped at his arms for warmth. "Please, sir, move along."

"I know the people who live here," I said, leaning over to the open window. "Are they all right?"

From the way he refused to look at me I knew the answer. I had a sudden vision of Simon standing in that door, Diane walking down the stairs. I wondered who had gone to break the news to Miss Simpson. Will grabbed my hand, and squeezed hard.

"It must have been some fire." His voice rose in question.

The cop shuffled his feet. He was obviously under orders not to talk to anyone, but his long vigil was lonely and boring. "Place was past saving by the time the alarm went out," he finally said.

"They heated with wood," I said before Will could stop me.

"That's it then," the constable nodded. He leaned on the car roof, bending down to speak across Will to me. "I had a chimney fire once at my old place. Damn scary. Lucky we were able to get it damped down before it set fire to the roof. If they were sound sleepers, they wouldn't even know what was happening. No sign of a smoke detector, anyway. You'd think people'd know better by now."

"When did it happen?"

"Yesterday afternoon, early evening. Listen, you're not the press, are you?" He peered into the car as if we might have a minicam hidden there, aimed at him and running. "There were lots of press out here last night, but it's so damn cold no one stuck around for long. I figured some of you would be back today. Chief told me to tell you to come downtown. There's nothing for you here." And he gestured at the ruin.

"The people who lived there — are you sure they were home at the time?" Perhaps Simon and Diane had gone into town themselves yesterday. I refused to think about the storm, how difficult driving out this road would have been.

"I'm sorry, but the people in there didn't have a chance. The coroner took out two bodies."

Another car pulled up behind us, a van emblazoned with the logo of the local TV station. The cop straightened up, smoothing his hands down the sleeves of his leather jacket. "You'd best go along," he said and turned to the newcomers.

"They were murdered," I said. Will kept driving, his attention on the road. I waited for him to deny my suspicion. He said nothing.

"And Rumble too. Maybe it wasn't suicide. I wish I'd noticed more. I wish I'd never found her." I turned up the heater, put the fan on full blast. Sadie's plaid blanket covered the back seat. I pulled it over and wrapped it around my legs, trying to get warm. I cupped my hands over my mouth and blew into them. Tears blurred my sight.

"I wonder if maybe you shouldn't tell Finlay you were there on Saturday," Will finally said.

"Why not?"

"It might look a bit strange, first you finding Rumble's

body and then turning up at the home of two of her close friends — friends who were working with her on some deal — the night before said friends get killed."

"You're not serious? Of course I have to tell them about the guy who came to the door, his argument with Simon. I'm sure now, it was that man I met in the park. Besides, I gave Constable Olan the address. They know already that I was there."

Will blew out a long sigh. "It'll mean more trouble."

"I know."

A white car was parked outside our house, belching exhaust into the clear air. I barely stepped out of the Honda when its driver slammed his door and stamped over to me.

"Where have you been?" Finlay shouted. He spat a wad of gum into the drift lining the gutter. "I thought you were so eager to see me today?"

"Look at that." I pointed to the lawn.

Finlay and Will both turned to see what I was pointing to. The snow lay fresh and undisturbed except for one path of footprints, the smooth track of a toboggan. We could hear the excited squeals of children sliding down the hill in the park. I knelt by the path, trying to decipher the stick message under the packed grooved trail.

"By the way," Finlay said quietly. "Where were you Saturday night?"

Will pulled me to my feet. "Let's go in," he suggested. "We've got a lot to talk about."

Finlay followed us up the steps. Will had his keys ready and opened the door, his hand ready to catch hold of Sadie before she ran out. I realized suddenly that I hadn't heard her barking.

Sadie didn't come to the door. She lay on the hall rug, still, her mouth open, her chest barely moving. Blood oozed from a wound on her head. Behind her, through the archway into the living room, I could see books spilled on the floor, the coffee table overturned.

Finlay pushed in past us, barely glancing at the dog. "Take her to the vet right now," he ordered Will. "And you," he pointed at me. "You stay here with me."

NINE

When I knelt down beside her, Sadie's eyes opened briefly, then rolled shut. Ignoring Finlay, I helped Will carry her out to the car, a dead weight, her legs and tail flopping against our thighs. She filled the whole back seat. I wanted to go with them.

"She'll be okay," Will said. He hugged me. I leaned into his embrace, not wanting to let go, to be let go.

"I'll call Dr. DuMaurier," I whispered. "I'll let her know you're coming. You'll phone me as soon as you can?"

Will nodded, and slipped into his seat. I slammed the door shut and walked slowly back up the path to the front door where Finlay was waiting.

"I'll need to use your phone," he said.

I led him into the kitchen. The phone receiver, knocked on to a heap of sugar and flour and beans, shrilled its distress. I phoned the vet first, then handed the receiver to Finlay who called in a report and requested a fingerprint unit to hurry over. While he talked, I surveyed the damage, stepping around pots and pans, broken dishes and spilled food to shut the refrigerator door. Egg shells, carrots and grapes floated on a sticky pool from which streamed milk and orange juice. Finlay wanted me to wait until the rest of his team arrived, but I couldn't stay still.

Each room had its own disaster: in the dining room, linens had been dumped from the sideboard while good dishes from the china cabinet were broken and strewn underfoot. The living room rug was hidden under a scatter of pillows, books, and record albums; cassettes had been emptied from their cases and crushed. The covers had been ripped from the stereo speakers and both the receiver and turntable were missing. I tripped over a lamp half hidden under the sofa cushions; the bulb shattered.

Upstairs was even worse. The bedroom had been torn apart, cupboards and drawers emptied, mattress ripped and torn from the bedframe, my jewellery box spilled on the mound of clothes and sheets. For once, I was glad that my earrings and necklaces had only sentimental value: on this first glance, nothing appeared to be missing. Most frightening of all was the hatred evident behind the destruction: a female corpse dangled from a gibbet carved into the wallpaper above the ruined bed.

My study was a blizzard of papers. The file cabinet drawers hung open, Will's records dumped and scattered over the floor. In the bathroom, the paraphernalia from the medicine chest lay broken and leaking all over the tub. Obscenities were scrawled on the mirror with face cream.

"What's missing?" Finlay had followed me through the house, watching, silent.

I just looked at him. I was afraid to open my mouth, had to keep swallowing to choke down the acid of anger and fear, my fists clenched and shirt soaked with sweat. The furnace roared. I slumped against the doorframe. Finlay reached for my arm, to give me some support, I would guess, but I shrugged him off. He followed me back downstairs where I lowered the thermostat before heading for the basement.

The TV was gone and so was the VCR. The sofabed had been pulled out and the mattress slashed open. Books had been ripped apart, Will's chess set smashed against the brick hearth of the woodstove which gaped wide, a fierce down draft chilling the room. In the cellar, the freezer had been left ajar, our winter's supply of beef and pork strewn on the floor. The door of the dryer swung open.

I began to pick up the pieces of meat, frost riming the pink butcher's paper. That was when I realized I was crying, tears running down my cheeks, splashing the packages as I placed them in orderly rows in the chest. I shivered constantly with cold. I kept rehearsing the steps I would have to take to get the house back into order, numbering lists whose beginnings I kept forgetting. I know I was talking out loud, my lips wet with tears that I rubbed off with the back of one hand.

The doorbell rang. A roast dropped to the floor. The wrapping split open and it rolled, raw and red, under the ironing board.

"That'll be McPhail," Finlay said as he headed for the stairs. I realized he had been standing behind me all the time. I bent to pick up the meat again, before going upstairs.

McPhail was a tall, muscular woman with a head of thick, blunt cut gray hair. She grasped my hand briefly in welcome and sympathy.

"Made a mess of it, eh?" she said. She waded through the litter in the living room and set her old-fashioned black medical bag down on the sofa. She snapped on a pair of thin plastic gloves, the kind a doctor wears. Her distinctive scent, an amalgam of chemicals, ivory soap, garlic and a fruity perfume combined with her black suit to give her the air of an undertaker. This impression was not lessened by the faint whistling she kept up as she walked through the house, methodically dusting some surfaces for prints but too often just shaking her head.

"Whoever did this would've worn gloves," she said, wiping off the residue of gray powder from the filing cabinet in the study. "Even kids know enough these days to do that. Television." She went to check the back door lock.

Two uniformed officers stood in the hall. Like children caught out in mischief, they stared down at their feet and didn't look me in the face even when I offered them my hand. I was the one who felt guilty, as if I had trashed my house myself.

"No sign of a break-in," said one.

"We keep an extra key in the garage. I locked myself out once and we thought we had found a good hiding place for it, above the door on the far side of a stud beam." I flushed when I saw the glance they exchanged, the rolled eyes.

"Someone probably saw you take it down and waited for a chance to use it." The same officer spoke.

"Will you make us a list of what's missing?" Finlay came up behind me. He jerked his head towards the kitchen and both constables left us.

I took his pen and notebook, replaced the cushions on the couch, and sat down to list what was obviously gone. Will had been at the vet's over an hour now. I didn't know if his long absence was a good sign or bad news.

He still wasn't back by the time the cops left. The two uniformed constables thought the break-in might be the work of a gang who had robbed several other houses in the neighbourhood. The key was missing from the garage and all the items stolen were easily sold.

"Kids looking for drug money," the spokesman said. "We see it all the time now, right?"

"I don't know," Finlay said. "It's too simple. I'll accept a coincidence here and there, but this is too much. Describe that man you saw in the park, see if any of these guys recognize him."

No one did.

"I saw him again two days ago," I continued. "That's why I've been trying to call you. He followed me from the Harper's on Saturday night and tried to run me off the road. Didn't you see the report from Olan and Leary? I asked them to make sure you got a copy."

"Harper," McPhail interrupted. "Isn't that the name of those people died in the fire up at the lake?"

"Shit," Finlay breathed. "I suppose you were going to call me about that, too?"

I nodded.

"That's out of our jurisdiction," the young cop volunteered. "The provincials have that one."

"Got a name?" Finlay snapped. When the other shook his head, he sighed. "It won't be hard to find out who's in charge. Find out and let me know, pronto." When the two cops hurried out, he turned back to me. "I suppose there's no way to persuade you to go on holiday until we get this straightened out? I'm kind of tired of seeing you turn up in all my cases."

"This is my home," I said. "I shouldn't be forced to leave my own house. By anyone."

"If anything else happens . . ." Finlay began, but was interrupted by the sudden insistent beeping of the radio he wore on his belt. "Damn. I've got to go." He ran a hand back over his skull. "You got someone can help you clear up this mess, stay with you until Mr. Cairns gets home? You shouldn't be alone."

"I'll call a friend," I said.

Finlay paused with his hand on the doorknob. "There'll be someone posted to keep an eye on your place. We can't afford round-the-clock protection but we'll keep close tabs." His beeper erupted again. "You take care now." He closed the door, but reopened it immediately. "I'm sorry about the dog. I hope she's okay."

"Right," I said. "Bye."

Will came home without Sadie. "She's going to be fine. She's got a slight concussion and needed stitches to close up the wound. Looks like she was hit by a baseball bat. But she's got a hard head, no permanent injury. Dr. DuMaurier wants to keep her in overnight for observation. She'll be home soon." He peered over my shoulder, assessing the damage.

"Karen's coming over to help," I told him. I blinked back tears.

"What's missing?"

"TV, VCR, stereo, camera."

"It's all covered by insurance then." He sighed, relieved.

"But look at this place. They even went through our drawers, all our clothes are tossed on the floor, wallpaper torn off the walls."

"You never liked that wallpaper anyway."

"My study's been destroyed, papers everywhere. Even my journal's been ripped up. I'm sure whoever it was read it. I feel so violated, so vulnerable."

"If it was kids, they probably can't read," Will tried to joke.

"What if it was that man from the park, looking for those papers everyone seems to think you have? That thing on the bedroom wall looks just like that sign I saw in the snow this morning."

"I wish I'd seen it too," Will said.

"You think I made it up?"

"No. I think the pressure is getting to you. You've been going through a rough time . . ."

"Give me a break. And what about Simon and Diane? The car that tried to run me off the road?"

"Coincidence."

"Even Finlay doesn't believe that any more." I stomped into the living room and began straightening the furniture. He followed, gathering up books and magazines.

"I think we should forget about what doesn't concern us. If — and I stress the if — it was your mystery man then he obviously now realizes you have nothing to hide. This place has been thoroughly turned over. And if it was kids, as the police did suggest, then we've just had some bad luck."

"Bad luck! What about Sadie?" I began to cry again.

Will tried to hug me, but I shrugged him off.

"I told you she'll be okay," he said. "Listen, let's get out of here, go downtown for something to eat. Maybe you could stay at Karen's tonight. I'll fix up a bed here in case the vet calls."

"I'm not hungry."

"I give up." Will threw down the magazines. "You don't want to even try to make things any easier, do you?"

"Anyone home?" Karen walked in, took one look at the room and at our faces and sat down abruptly on the arm of the sofa. "What a disaster. I can see why you missed the meeting."

"Meeting? What meeting?" I asked.

"At the store with Dr. Long."

"I forgot all about it." I flopped down beside her, my head in my hands. "I don't even want to think about it, but I better ask what happened."

"We all had our say and Dr. Long said she'd think it over and call later this week. Lil fell apart though. She was trying to explain her plan about children's authors and started to dither and get things mixed up. I think she was really expecting you to be there."

"Well, I wasn't." I rubbed my eyes savagely.

"I'm sure the doctor will make the right decision," Will tried to be soothing.

"What do you know about it?" I retorted. "What about Stephanie?"

"She was almost as bad. She couldn't decide which angle would impress Long more: the struggling single mother, the long-working employee, the ambitious career woman. She kept switching from one to the other, always in a most reasonable tone. As if she took it for granted that she would get the job and was just going through the motions."

"And what did the good doctor have to say?"

"Not much. She asked where you were and I told her you had an appointment you couldn't miss. I reminded her you'd been there as long as Stephanie had. She's seen the order books; she knows you do most of that work."

"Oh well. At the moment the store doesn't seem to matter very much." I looked around. "Can I stay at your place tonight, Karen?"

She glanced at Will and then back to me. "Sure. Are you sure?"

"Yeah."

Will went into the kitchen. We heard him tossing broken crockery into a bag.

"Okay." Karen slapped her knees and stood up. "Look at it this way: early spring cleaning."

A crash and a curse sent us running to the kitchen. Will lay on his back in the spilled flour, his hair dusted in a parody of old age. A smear of butter showed where he had skidded, the canister of sugar he'd been carrying still sifting powder.

"You look ridiculous." Karen exploded in giggles which she tried to smother with one hand. "Are you all right?"

"Laugh at me, eh?" Will roared. He grabbed a handful of rice from a small heap by the cupboards and threw it at her, the grains catching in her hair. She retaliated with a squirt from a bottle of lemon juice.

"Food fight," she shrieked. I watched them for a moment but my anger couldn't hold. The room was such a mess anyway. The ketchup lay on its side on the counter. I shook it up well and let fly, hitting both of them. The battle was on.

The food fight made cleaning the kitchen simpler: we swept everything into garbage bags. Karen left to get pizza and some beer. The closing door was a signal: Will found me on my knees in the bedroom, sorting torn clothes. Without a word, he hugged me; after a moment, I hugged back.

About midnight, Karen stuffed the last book into the shelf in the living room. "That's it for tonight," she sighed. "I'm beat."

I sat cross-legged on the floor surrounded by cassettes and their boxes, trying to fit them together.

"Are you coming back with me?" she asked.

"No," I said.

"Good." She stretched. "Everything will be okay." She

shouted good-bye to Will who was working upstairs and let herself out. "I'll be back in the morning," she called.

Will carried two bulging plastic bags downstairs.

"I guess we might as well quit for now too," I said.

He had made up the mattress on the floor, in a corner beside the window. The blinds were a tangle of cords and slats that would take hours to unravel. I tried hanging towels across the panes. They wouldn't stay up without nails and neither of us wanted to go down to the basement to try to find the hammer. We undressed in the dark and slipped under the sleeping bag we were using to replace the duvet which had shed feathers everywhere. We lay stiff, side by side, not touching. The ceiling high above us wavered with shadows.

"This is getting serious," Will said.

"I know."

"I wish there was something I could do."

"I wish I'd never gone down to the river that day."

We lay still a moment longer, then hand reached out to hand. For a very long time we clung together, not sleeping.

When Karen arrived the next morning, she lugged in a portable colour TV. "Mom gave this to me to lend to you," she said. "It's from her cottage. She doesn't like to leave it up there over the winter, afraid the picture tube will freeze, or something like that. It'll probably take the insurance company a few weeks to pay up, so you might find it useful. How's Sadie?"

"The vet's going to keep her for a couple of days," Will replied. "She's got a bad concussion, still can't stand without support."

Karen plugged in the TV. "Right. Where do we begin?"

Will left after lunch for a meeting he couldn't afford to miss. Karen and I took a break, lounging on the couch, its cushions stained but presentable. She fiddled with the TV's antennae, and tuned in a soap opera, a close-up of a couple clinched in a long wet kiss.

"So, how's Will?" she asked.

"Busy."

"He says you're thinking of going away for a few days. A holiday."

"He's the one thinks I should go. So does Finlay. Me, I'm not ready to run away yet. I don't even know what I'm running from. Or to."

"Rosie, what's really going on? With you and Will I mean? Do you think he had an affair with Jennifer Rumble?"

"Of course not," I snapped. I couldn't meet her eyes. "He wouldn't lie to me. And I would know if he'd been seeing someone else, he'd give it away in the way he behaved. I've known him for so long, I know how he acts. Anyway, with his business he doesn't have time for the dog, not to mention me or anyone else."

"But it's funny, don't you think?" Karen persisted. "Jennifer Rumble must have come to town to meet someone. The papers she had with her are gone; someone must have them. And the only person she knew in town, according to the Harpers and your Mystery Man, was Will."

"He doesn't deny that he knew her," I said. "He just says he hasn't seen her in years, that they were acquaintances, that's all."

"The Harpers are dead."

"You don't have to remind me," I shivered.

"They're the only ones Will could have confronted to get at the truth. Unless the other guy comes forward."

"You don't think he exists either, do you?"

"Someone did this." She waved one hand around the room.

"Dunstable," I said suddenly. "He's connected to all this too. He said that he worked with her on some kind of refugee program. So maybe he's got her papers."

"Why would he come to see you then? You'd think he'd try

to keep a low profile if he had anything to do with her death."

"You think Dunstable had an affair with her?" In spite of ourselves, we began to giggle. The thought of Dunstable engaged in a passionate embrace was too ludicrous to bear.

"What about a private detective?" Karen finally suggested.

"A private detective?"

"Sure. For my sake, a Sam Spade, not a Benny Cooperman."

"You're nuts," I said. I stood up. "We'd better get back to work."

"Wait a minute, Rosie, I'm serious about this. You need someone to look into Rumble's past, sordid or not. See if she was the selfless crusader for refugees that Will claims she was or whether she's some kind of blackmailer."

"Come off it," I said. "You're being too dramatic."

"Look at the facts, ma'am," Karen mimicked Jack Webb. She sat up straighter, numbering her fingers as she spoke. "The Harpers came to town looking for Rumble's stuff. They asked you out to their place to question you about her and Will. Simon said he was afraid that her papers might make Diane out to be an addict, perhaps a criminal. They're both killed before you or the police can question them any further."

"That was an accident. A chimney fire. Although it wouldn't surprise me if Mystery Man, as you call him, had something to do with it."

"So consider him too. He's also anxious to find those papers, even went into the river at this time of year to look for them. He's threatened you and trashed your house -- at least, you seem to think he's the one who's responsible for this. He's pretty serious about getting them back, I'd say. Maybe he thinks she's got some secrets in her diary about him too."

I circled the rim of my tea cup with one finger, considering Karen's words.

She paused for only a minute before continuing. "From how you described his behaviour, Dunstable seems terribly upset about what she might have written about him and his church. As if he knew she could cause trouble if whatever she wrote became public. Maybe she had something on Will too."

"I thought Will was your friend."

"He is. But so are you. And wondering about all this is tearing you apart. I can see it. I know you're afraid he might be hiding something. A private detective could make some inquiries for you, maybe find out who the Mystery Man is so you can identify him to the police."

"I couldn't afford it," I said.

"How do you know?"

"Isn't it always a hundred dollars a day plus expenses?" I retorted. "I don't have that kind of money. And I couldn't borrow it from Will without him asking a lot of questions."

"Why don't you just call an agency and ask for an estimate?"

I shook my head. "I couldn't go behind Will's back like that. If he ever found out, he'd be furious. Besides, I trust him. I really do. Whatever's going on, he's an innocent part of it."

"Is it because you're afraid of the answers that you won't ask any questions?" Karen demanded.

"That's not fair," I said. "Let's not talk about it any more, or I'll have to get angry at you. Will's my husband. I love him and I believe him. That's all there is to it."

"I think you're crazy not to get someone to investigate this for you," Karen said.

"There's a lot of craziness going around," I answered. A sudden burst of music drew our attention to the set. A woman was waltzing in an enormous kitchen with a mop. "Back to the salt mines. You do the study and I'll tackle the laundry room."

By the time Karen left at five, we'd managed to clear away the worst mess. The kitchen was usable again. Will phoned to say he was at a crucial point with taping wallboard and wouldn't be back until late. He'd eat at Jerry's and drive the truck home. I didn't want to stay in the house alone. In spite of our argument, I called Karen and she invited me over.

Karen's apartment was on the second floor of an old house built in the days of large families and live-in servants. Years ago, the house had been divided into six flats, two on each floor. Karen's consisted of a large sitting room whose bay window looked out over the courthouse lawn, a small bedroom, a bathroom with a shower stall instead of a tub, and a kitchen just big enough to include a pine table and two cane-seated chairs. An iron fire escape served as a balcony and back entrance. The yard below it had been converted to parking for the tenants' cars.

I planned to leave my own car in back in Karen's spot, rather than look for parking on the street. I didn't relish a long walk in the cold dark and there was no parking allowed on the blocks around the courthouse. Karen kept her old Volkswagen in the garage at her mother's house which was only three blocks away, close enough to soothe Mrs. Lewis's anxieties about not seeing her daughter, but far enough away to give Karen some feeling of independence.

I turned off Court Avenue into the alley that gave access to the garages and backyards. Without streetlights and bordered by high wooden fences, it felt like entering a tunnel. I parked between a pickup truck and a station wagon. From the next yard, a large dog began to bark wildly. I thought of Sadie. As I bent to lock the door, I caught movement in the shadows under the fire stairs.

I stood up quickly and arranged the keys in my fist, points out. "Who's there?" I called.

No one answered.

My mother always said I have too much imagination, I reminded myself. All the first floor rooms of the neighbouring houses were dark. Karen's kitchen light was on, but she was likely in the living room waiting for me to ring at the front door. The wind blew the tail of my scarf up over my face.

A person stepped out of the shadows: short and slight, bundled in a black greatcoat, the face covered by a dark balaclava. I pulled at the car door handle, forgetting that I'd just locked it, the keys in my other hand. The person giggled, shrill and wild.

"What do you want?" I quavered. The swing of a hand raised high, the poise of the body made me think it must be a man.

Headlights illuminated the alley. My would-be attacker cursed and fled. I stumbled across the frozen ruts of the drive. The fire escape had not been shovelled. I hauled myself up the slippery steps by clinging to the railing. It seemed to take a very long time for Karen to answer my knocks at her back door. I kept glancing down into the shadows of the fence, but the man did not come back.

"What are you doing back here?" Karen demanded. She had pulled back the blind that covered the window and was peering at me through the crack.

"Open up. Hurry."

I heard the slide and crash of a bolt being drawn back and then I fell into the welcome warm light of the kitchen.

Karen slammed the door shut. "What happened to you? You look like you've seen a ghost."

"Some guy tried to attack me."

"In the yard?"

I nodded. "When I got out of the car. He was by your staircase. Almost as if he were waiting for me." I shivered.

Karen reached over my shoulder to slam the bolt home. "Are you okay?"

"Yeah." I got to my feet, rubbing at bruises on my knees.

"I'll call the police, then."

"No. Don't." I grabbed her arm as she lifted the phone from its cradle on the wall by the door.

"Why not?"

"I just can't handle any more of this," I said. "Maybe this is the first real coincidence. I didn't get a good look at the guy, but he seemed a lot younger and a lot smaller than that other man."

"You're serious?" Karen took her hand away from the phone and hugged me. "Shouldn't we at least call Finlay?"

"No. He'll just tell me I should get out of town for awhile."

"That's not a bad idea," Karen murmured. She tugged me gently into the living-room.

"Not you too," I sighed. "Why won't you all just leave me alone?"

"Because we care about you."

"If you cared about me, you'd give me something to drink. Something strong."

"Sit down then." Karen pushed me in the direction of the futon couch and disappeared back into the kitchen.

It was a long way down. I stretched out my legs, leaned my head back against the rough Mexican blanket that served as a wall hanging, covering the flowered wallpaper that Karen couldn't be bothered to replace. In front of me was a large framed print of Picasso's "Woman With A Book." I sympathized with her fractured shape. One of Karen's three cats, a long-haired calico named Emily (for Dickinson), slid off the couch. She stalked towards the bedroom but stopped in the middle of the room to wash one paw. I called to her, but she ignored me.

Bamboo beads jangled as Karen swept through them from the kitchen. She handed me a glass of white wine, placed the bottle on the floor beside me. "I know I should be giving you brandy but this is all I've got in the house."

I sipped gingerly. It wasn't too bad. Karen usually bought Niagara wine, she said to support the local industry. Sometimes her finds were like acidic fruit juice. This one at least left no aftertaste.

Karen nested on a pile of varicolored pillows that made a colourful splash on the varnished hardwood floor. The cat joined her. The only other furniture in the room was a large table she used for a desk and a straight chair that matched the ones in her kitchen.

Books were stacked on brick and board shelves along one long wall; plants filled the floor in front of the bay window which was curtained by a plain rice paper blind she seldom bothered lowering. She wore a long, heavily embroidered caftan she had brought back from her travels. She tucked her bare feet under her.

"You could be right about that guy who accosted you, that he had nothing to do with this other business. You know Cindy who lives upstairs? She told me she saw some boy coming down the fire escape yesterday. She shouted and he took off. She knows I don't always bolt the back door, it's such a hassle to undo all the locks to let the cats in and out. The landlord's promised to gate the bottom of the back stairs so no one can get up them, but of course he hasn't done anything yet. We've worked out a system to keep watch for each other. When it's time for you to leave, I'll ask her friend Gary to walk you down to the car."

Gossip was a welcome antidote to fear. I took her up on it. "Is Gary living with her now?"

For over a year, Karen's upstairs neighbour had provided us with a live soap opera. Cindy Reed was a seventeen-year-old high-school drop-out. She worked sporadically as a waitress in one or other of the fast food restaurants that shared the highway strip at the town limits with car lots and gas stations. In between jobs, she collected unemployment and hung out with her friends in the malls.

Karen befriended her, tried to persuade her to go back to school, at least to take night courses. Cindy had almost agreed when she met Gary Donnelly, an ex-con who worked for his uncle pumping gas in a station along the strip. Now that he had moved in with her, she was no longer interested in school of any kind.

"It's too bad," Karen said. "She's really a bright kid, but she's never had a break. She hinted to me once that her father abused her. Her mother comes around once in awhile, but they just argue. Her Mom wants her back in school and away from Gary."

"Do you think it's good for her to be with him?"

Karen shrugged. "I hardly know him. He seems all right. At least since he's been with her, she's been working steadily, not drinking so much. I was getting tired of coming up with excuses not to buy booze for her. I didn't want her mad at me, but I couldn't stand to see her drunk."

I put down my glass. The bottle was already half empty. "What's on the tube tonight?" I asked.

"Want to watch a movie? I've got the video of *Fatal Attraction.*"

Movies and television were Karen's greatest vice. She had a twenty-eight inch colour set and VCR on a small table in her bedroom. I brought the bottle and glasses and we both plumped down on the waterbed. Karen had one rule for watching movies: no comments could be made until the film was over, although laughter and groans were allowed in small measure. When the music began, Emily jumped up to sit on Karen and another cat, a delicate orange tiger, appeared to curl by my side. As usual, the third, a pure black neutered tom, was nowhere in sight. He didn't like visitors.

Glenn Close was waiting, knife in hand, for Michael Douglas to come back home when someone began to pound on the back door. Both cats went flying as Karen and I leaped off the bed.

"There's a car on fire," a man shouted. "Call 911."

I looked out the kitchen window. Black smoke trailed up, obscuring the roof of my Honda.

TEN

We didn't bother with coats. Karen wrenched open the door and I stumbled after the man down the frozen steps while she dialled for help. In the light spilling from the kitchen, I could see a pony tail flapping against broad shoulders clad in a denim jacket as he half-hopped, half-slid down the packed steps. Behind me, lighter footsteps descended

"Be careful, Gare," a young woman called out. She slipped and bumped into me. I clutched the railing. She clung to my sleeve. For a moment, we tottered. I steadied, she let go, and we took the rest of the descent more slowly.

Gary approached the car cautiously. He picked up a deadfall branch and poked at the twisted cloth that hung from the gas valve which had been forced open. The cap to the gas tank had been left sitting on the roof. There were no flames; greasy black smoke smouldered from embers along the outer edges of the rag. Gary hooked it and pulled it away from the car. He stamped on it, viciously, as if it were a snake. The stink of gasoline smothered the yard.

Sirens now joined the strangled yelping of the dog next door. A couple of doors slammed, people coming out to find the source of the commotion. Karen brought me my coat. It didn't do much to help quell my shivers.

A police car pulled up behind the fire engines. Big men in heavy black raincoats and knee-high boots tumbled from the trucks and clustered around the smoking rag, the scorched trunk.

"Good work," one said to Gary. "If the flames got to the tank, she would have blown."

He shrugged, and turned to go back upstairs.

"Wait a minute," a cop said. "Don't I know you?"

"Leave him alone," Cindy shouted. "Can't you give a guy a break?"

All the men ignored her. Gary didn't seem to mind the cold. He pointed up to the third floor apartment and kicked at the rag with one booted foot.

"They need to find out what happened," Karen soothed. "We all know that it's nothing to do with him. He's the hero here."

"Yeah," Cindy muttered. "They'll make him mad. You just watch, he'll take off any minute now."

The cop flipped his notebook closed and turned towards us. Gary stared at his back a moment, then headed towards the street. "I told you," Cindy hissed. She dropped her cigarette and raced after him.

"Constable Mitchell," the young man touched his cap briefly as he introduced himself. "You know who owns this vehicle?"

"It's mine." I came closer, trying to assess the damage. The fire truck emitted a high-pitched beep as it backed out of the drive and down the alley.

"Lucky the only damage was to the paint," Mitchell continued. "You can get the gas cap back on for now. You better see about getting the lock replaced right away. You know why someone would want to do this to you?"

"No."

Karen interrupted. "You should call Constable Finlay, he knows all about the case."

"What case?"

"Never mind," I said. I pushed Karen towards the stairs, none too gently. "Can't we go inside if we have to talk?" I continued. "It's freezing out here and I have to phone my husband to tell him I'll be late."

We trooped up to Karen's apartment. I tried to call Will. He wasn't answering his phone. That wasn't unusual when he was engrossed in the computer, but I wished that for once he had remembered to leave his answering machine turned on.

"Why your car?" Mitchell asked me when I finally hung up. "Why choose your car out of all the cars parked back there?"

"I don't know." I was so tired. "Maybe he likes red cars."

"Didn't you have a break-in at your house yesterday?"

I nodded. He must be one of the policemen who responded to Finlay's call. All the young ones looked alike to me.

"He could've thought it was Gary's car," Karen suggested. "He used to drive an old Camarro, a red one. He traded it in for a new 4x4 last week."

"Even in the dark, it would be hard to mistake a Honda for a Camarro," Mitchell shook his head.

"There was someone in the yard when I parked." I told him about the figure in the balaclava, the threat implied in his behaviour. He wrote down every word.

"Why didn't you report this?" he asked when I finished.

I was saved from having to answer by a voice that boomed and echoed in the closed space of the yard.

"Hey, Mark. Where are you? Look what I found."

Mitchell peered out the window. "It's Adams. He's got someone. You better come with me."

A second police car had pulled up behind the first, its red and blue lights revolving. In the alternating glare and shadow, we saw Cindy and Gary return. He held a cigarette up as if to hide his face while she hung on his arm, urging him towards the fire escape and the safety of their home.

Adams fit the stereotype of a jock gone to seed. He was tall with wide shoulders that hunched over a belly that strained the zipper of his navy parka. His cap was pushed to the back of his head over hair combed straight back from a low, corrugated forehead. His nose had been broken at least once. He puffed on a short cigar, its foul smoke mingling with the odour of singed paint and oil. When he saw us coming, he flipped the butt into the nearest snowbank.

"Any of you seen this guy before?" He reached in the open window and pulled on the collar of his prisoner's jacket, half hauling him out the window. It was a boy, younger than Cindy, his face twisted in a sneer, his dark hair cut close except for one long lock that fell over his left eye. One ear was pierced with a blue stone and a long dangling feather. A black knit hat was stuffed in one pocket. It could have been the balaclava.

"That's the kid I saw on the fire escape," Cindy volunteered.

"So, Matty," the big cop said, thrusting the boy back inside. "You just can't keep out of trouble can you? What do you think your old man will have to say this time?"

"Is he the one you saw earlier?" Mitchell asked me.

"Could be," I answered. "The person was small and wearing dark clothes, but I couldn't see his face for the ski mask and he didn't say anything."

"What about you?" He turned to Gary. "Is this the guy you saw down in the parking lot before the fire?"

The boy spoke for the first time. "Recognize me, do you?" he dared.

Gary wouldn't meet his gaze. "Same as her. He was all dressed in dark clothes, moved fast. Looked like a kid, but . . ."

"We'll take him in anyway," Adams decided. "He was hanging around, made a run for it when we spotted him. Maybe he'll have something to say for himself after he's sat in a cell a bit. Wouldn't be the first time for fun and games for this boy now, would it?" He punched the boy, not lightly, on the shoulder. "A real little juvenile delinquent, aren't we? As for you folks, there's no point in coming downtown with us if you can't make an i.d. Unless you want to lay trespassing charges, lady?" he asked Cindy.

She shook her head.

The boy grinned. "Smart dame," he said.

"What's his name?" Karen asked.

"Him?" The man jerked a thumb at the backseat. "Matthew Mark Dunstable."

"Dunstable's son?" I wondered when we were alone again. "Do you think he could have been after me?"

"How would he know you'd be at my house?" Karen countered. "Maybe he's seen me in the store and has a thing for older women."

"It's nothing to joke about."

"I know, I know. It sounded like the cops knew him, that he's been in trouble before. You know, the classic son-of-a-preacher syndrome, real hell-raiser. He probably picked this house by chance, no lights on downstairs so it looked like easy pickings. Maybe he was on the stairs when you drove in and thought that if he frightened you, he'd be able to get away."

"He did that all right. But why would he come back? Why torch my car?"

"To get even? Because you kept him from breaking in?"

"He seemed pretty sure of himself. He scared Cindy anyway."

"Or Gary. I got the feeling he knew the kid. He's still on probation and the less he has to do with the police the better. That's probably why he wouldn't identify him. He's making a real effort to keep out of trouble. Cindy says."

"She really loves him."

"Yeah. I'm a little worried about that. He's at least ten years older than she is. And with a pretty long record. Well, if his own uncle will give him a chance in a job, who am I to say that he's not straightening up?"

I rubbed at the goose bumps on my arms. "Did you see the look on that boy's face? He looked so mean, so contemptuous."

"He knows his father will get him out of jail and he'll be right back on the street. And the next car he tries to fix, he probably will blow. Cindy's not stupid enough not to know that and to know the cops and Gary can't keep watch forever. She's probably worried he would take revenge if she did i.d. him."

"How did you get to be such an expert on crime?"

She pointed to the TV. "The tube never lies. Seriously, I used to see kids like him all the time out in Vancouver, living on the streets. At least he's still at home."

"I wouldn't want to be Dunstable's kid."

"Neither does he."

"Do you think he's the one who broke into our house too?"

"Not likely. The Dunstables live around here somewhere. Across the river is alien turf. He wouldn't go over there unless he had a good reason."

"I guess." I didn't want to think about the boy or his motivations any more. "Will's going to have a fit when he sees the car."

"He'll be glad that you weren't in it."

"He'll say I should have stayed home. That it's my fault somehow."

"It could have been anyone's car. The Dunstable kid was just out to raise trouble, and you happened to get into his way. That's what Will will say. You know that."

"Now you've got excuses for him?" I acccused her. "I thought you thought he was being blackmailed by Jennifer Rumble, that he murdered her and the Harpers."

"I was just playing devil's advocate," Karen sniffed. "You know I couldn't really believe that of Will."

"You have no idea what he's really like."

"And you do?"

"We've been married fifteen years."

"And I've known both of you for twenty years, remember. What's with the two of you lately? You really don't believe he has anything to do with all this, do you?"

I tipped the bottle, pouring the last of the wine into my glass. "I've been thinking about that argument we had. Tell me the truth. Do you believe he was sleeping with Jennifer Rumble?"

"Will? You must be joking. He's the most married man I've ever known. Besides which, he's hopeless at keeping anything secret. Like your birthday present last year, remember?"

"I'm serious, Karen."

"So am I. If Will had an affair, it would be because he'd fallen out of love with you. And if that happened, he wouldn't lie about it and stay with you. You know that. You wouldn't do it either. He hardly knew Jennifer Rumble. He only mentioned her name because you found her body."

"That's what he says."

"Don't you trust him?"

I shrugged. "We hardly talk any more."

"Whose fault is that?"

I wanted to answer "his." I wanted to complain about all his late night work, his hurried departures. I could feel the whine rising in my throat. I shook my head. Even from my best friend, our best friend, some things were better kept private.

"I'd hate to see anything happen to you two," Karen continued when I said nothing. "Sometimes, I just want to take you by the shoulders and shake some sense into you, both of you, show you what's at stake. Love and all that."

All that, I thought on my careful drive home, is what worries me.

It was a beautiful morning, the sun high and white, the trees bowing under fresh snow, each twig coated and glistening. Will and I stood side by side staring at the car parked in the driveway. He rubbed the scorch mark on the fender with his bare thumb. Flakes of red paint fell away. He slapped the roof. "This has gone far enough. I think Dunstable owes us an apology. And his kid owes us for a paint job."

"We don't know for sure that he did it. The police found him hanging around, but then he does live in the neighbourhood. Maybe he was curious to see what all the fuss was about."

"The cops took him in though. They knew who he was."

"He'd been in trouble before. Petty theft."

"Our break-in?"

"I wondered about that too."

"I'll call Finlay, see if the kid confessed, if there's any connection."

Will stamped back in the house. In a few minutes, we could go and bring Sadie home. I fingered the rawhide bone in my pocket, a toy to cheer her up. In spite of last night's misadventures and Will's anger, I couldn't keep from smiling, my face lifted to the light, eyes closed, breathing deeply in the crisp air. Crows called to each other from the tops of spruce trees. A tingle of woodsmoke wafted down from a neighbour's chimney.

"He's on leave. And no one else is willing to discuss the case with me."

"Let's just go get the dog."

Will said little on the drive to the vet's office, but Sadie's enthusiastic welcome melted his frustration. She danced around us, tail wagging furiously, her tongue reaching for our faces. We fended her off, laughing. She went from one to the other of us, her jaws gripping our forearms lightly in greeting. She couldn't get out of the building fast enough.

We took her for a long walk in the park before returning home. Now she slept, stretched out her full length on the living room rug, her paws twitching in a dream of rabbits.

"I can't stand waiting any longer for Finlay to phone." Will put down the sheaf of plans he'd been checking. "Let's call on the Dunstables."

"You think we should?"

"I think we deserve some explanation."

"Let me phone first."

My call wasn't answered. Will went back to his drawings and I made up my mind to strip the rest of the wallpaper in our bedroom. It had to be done, sooner or later, before we could begin to repaint the room. And it was a perfect chore for a time like this: a mindless labour, a matter of scrubbing and scraping, an antidote to worry. Every little while, I stopped to dial the Dunstable's number. It wasn't answered until after supper.

"Yeah?" It was a young man's voice, cocky and belligerent.

"Is Ian Dunstable home?" I asked.

"Who's asking?"

"I'd like to speak to him."

"He's not here. You the one who's been phoning all day? Driving my mother crazy?"

"I really do have to talk to Mr. Dunstable. Perhaps you could tell me where he is?"

Over the hum of static on the line, I heard a thin and quavery voice in the background. "Is it church business, Matty? Ask them to call Mr. Philpott."

"Shut up, Ma." The boy swore under his breath, then spoke to me. "You're that bookstore bitch, aren't you? My father wants nothing to do with you and neither do the rest of us. You keep away from us and maybe you won't have any more trouble."

"Matty, what are you saying?" The woman's voice was clearer this time, as if she had come right up to the phone and was standing at her son's elbow.

I called out, "Mrs. Dunstable, I'd like to speak to you. Please."

The receiver clicked down on the sound of their argument.

Will left early next morning on a job he couldn't delay. I had to work in the afternoon, so I decided to call on Mrs. Dunstable myself. Will wanted us to go together; I was just as anxious to go alone. He seldom lost his temper; in fact, he had the reputation of being a quiet, reserved man, but when he did get angry, he could be loud and abrasive. I thought that Mrs. Dunstable might be more willing to speak to a woman alone.

The house was on a side street not far from Karen's flat. Set back from the sidewalk, it was a tall, narrow, three-storey building whose front windows were heavily curtained. A line of discoloured brick arching across the facade was the only evidence that a roofed verandah had once graced the house, softening its lines. Now the walk ended in a set of concrete steps, severely trimmed yews bordering the foundation.

There was no bell, so I pulled on the storm door. It was locked. I banged on the glass but was sure that the solid oak door behind it absorbed all sound. I thought I saw the curtain twitch and leaned over the iron railing to knock on the picture window. No answer.

A clean-swept path led around the side of the house. I followed it to the back door and knocked again. A blind hid the interior and I couldn't tell if this door opened into a mud room or the kitchen itself.

I thought about giving up and going home. Whoever was inside obviously didn't want visitors. The snow in the backyard was a maze of footsteps leading to a garage and another alley. I looked at the lawn more closely. Someone had practiced drawing stick figures, a hangman as in the childhood game, as in the sign I'd seen outside my own front door and carved into my bedroom wall. I marched back to the front of the house and began to drum on the glass.

"I know you're home," I shouted. "I'll stay here until you let me in or until all your neighbours come out to see what's going on."

The inside door opened slowly. Mrs. Dunstable was a thin, small woman. Her gray hair was skewered so tightly into a knot covered with black net that the skin of her face looked as if it had been stretched to the breaking point to cover her skull. Her eyelids, red with weeping, drooped over green eyes above a narrow, turned-up nose, and pale, bitten lips. A bruise blossomed on one temple.

"Come in, then," she whispered, looking over my shoulder up the street. "But you can't stay long."

The house smelled of floor wax and bacon. The hall was dark, uncarpeted. Mrs. Dunstable made no move to take my jacket, so I draped it over the newel post.

"Give me your boots," she ordered, her voice tense and strained.

I slipped them off and handed them to her. She held them up to the light from the low-wattage fixture that hung from the high ceiling.

"Good boots," she nodded. "Sensible."

"I do a lot of walking," I said. "The rubber soles keep the water out and the leather keeps my ankles warm."

"I have the same kind." She placed them side by side on a newspaper spread over a grate by the front door. "We can talk in here." She led the way into the living room.

She had been polishing the oak floor. A rug was rolled up in the archway to the dining room which was stuffed with a long green velour sofa, a matching loveseat, a round oak pedestal table, and six heavily carved chairs. Even my stockinged footsteps raised echoes in the bare room. The only pictures on the wall were a family photograph taken when their son appeared an angelic child and a crucifix painted in medical detail. The room was cold but stuffy, as if the windows were never opened. The drapes were still tightly drawn.

"I'm Rosalie Cairns," I held out my hand in greeting.

She ignored my gesture. She stood with her arms crossed, hands clutching her elbows in claws whose knuckles gleamed. She wore a long, faded blue apron over a flowered housedress, her bare feet stuffed into blue knitted slippers.

"I know who you are," she said, her voice so low that I had

to lean forward to hear her. "What do you want with me?"

"I just want to talk to your husband."

"He's not here."

"Perhaps you could tell me where to find him?"

She turned away, the fingers of her left hand fluttering for an instant over the bruised cheekbone. "I don't know."

"Are you in some kind of trouble, Mrs. Dunstable?" I spoke as gently as I could. Her hand dropped down as if stung and when she looked at me, her face was flushed, her eyes bright and glistening.

"It's none of your business. None of this is your business. It's people like you who go round causing trouble for the rest of us. Matty thought you'd be around. He told me you blamed him for that trouble the other night. Everyone picks on my boy. I have nothing to say to you. Now, or ever. I'd like you to leave me and my family alone. Go away, and don't come back."

"Please listen to me. Your husband appears to be involved in something pretty nasty. A lot of bad things have been happening. Scary things. People have died, I've been attacked, my house has been ransacked. He came to see me the other day. I think he knows why all these things have been happening to me. I have a right to know whatever it is."

Matty Dunstable barged into the room. "Whydja let her in the house? She's trouble, I tolja."

He looked as if he hadn't slept well. His eyes were circled by rings of exhaustion he reddened further by rubbing one fist into them. His hair stuck up all over his head in tangled greasy spikes and when he yawned, a wave of foul breath washed over us. He wore gray track pants that drooped from his hips. His thin bare chest was white and hairless. When he scratched his ribs, red stripes appeared over the ridges of bone.

"I had to let her in," his mother whined. "She was making such a racket, banging on the door. The neighbours would hear."

"Whadja tell her?" The boy raised his hand and the woman

flinched, her fingers darting back to the bruise.

"Nothing," I broke in. "She said nothing to me. I just want to talk to your father."

"Get me breakfast." The boy gestured toward the kitchen and Mrs. Dunstable, sniffling, scurried away. He snorted, rubbed his hand across his nose and then across the seat of his pants. "He's not around, hasn't been around for a coupla days. Ma hadda come down to the cop shop to spring me. Didn't like that much, did she?" He laughed outright, "Scared you, din't I?"

"It was you, then? You tried to set fire to my car? Why?"

He scratched his testicles, letting his hand cradle them long enough to get my attention. Then he grinned. "That would be telling. My lawyer says, I'm not supposed to talk."

"Who's your lawyer?"

He yawned. "A guy. None of your beeswax, unless you got evidence. And that you don't have, right?"

"Clever, aren't you?" I stared him in the eyes until he looked away.

"What's taking you, Ma?" he yelled towards the kitchen. A pot clattered to the floor. He hitched up his pants and turned back to me. "Whadja want with my old man? Gonna tell on me?"

"It's got nothing to do with you. I hope."

"Well, he ain't here."

"Do you have any idea where he might be?"

"Last I heard, he went t' chapel. New place out onna highway. Hasn't been home since. Good riddance." He wiped his nose again with the back of his hand.

"Matthew, your breakfast." Mrs. Dunstable appeared in the door, a cup of coffee steaming in one hand, a plate laden with bacon, eggs and toast in the other.

"I'm not hungry any more." The boy brushed past her up the stairs, knocking the cup from her hands.

Coffee splashed to the floor, barely missing her slippered foot. She said nothing. She didn't move. The plate in her other hand drooped, and food slipped off to join the puddle. I realized she was weeping, tears streaming down her face. Upstairs, a door slammed and pipes shrieked once as a shower was turned on in company with a blast of heavy metal music.

"Is there anything I can do?" I reached to touch her.

She recoiled. My hand hesitated, then dropped. She balanced the empty cup carefully on the plate and pulled a balled handkerchief from her apron pocket.

"Can't you see you've done enough?" she spat. "Just leave."

I stood still for a moment, then went to get my coat and boots. As I let myself out the front door, she was still standing over the spilled food, rocking back and forth, wrapped in her own arms. I thought I could hear her humming but the clamour of music and pouring water from the bathroom upstairs obscured the tune. I closed the door gently and walked away from there as quickly as I could.

ELEVEN

"There you are. At last." Stephanie put on her coat as I came in the door. She wore a blue tweed dress suit, and her hair had recently been permed into a mass of tight curls. "I'm going to be late," she added. There were four customers in the store; one of the women glanced our way. Stephanie lowered her voice. "I'm meeting Dr. Long for lunch. She's going to tell me her decision."

"What's been decided?" I paused at the door to take my boots off.

"She hasn't said anything yet. But I think I can guess." She smiled.

"That's odd." I went to the basement stairs and hung my coat on one of the hooks on the landing.

"What?"

"She called me too. She's dropping in to the store about three. After your lunch, I guess."

"She'll want to tell you herself."

"Maybe. Has she spoken to Lil, do you know?"

"Lil doesn't want the job. I talked it over with her, and Fred agreed with me that she just wasn't suited. She's too nervous, gets too upset over small things to handle the responsibility."

"Well, thanks for consulting me," I retorted. The basement door slammed much louder than I expected. The two girls in the far corner of the store by the romance racks stopped giggling for a moment.

Stephanie adjusted the knot of the fringed shawl she draped

over one shoulder. "We had a meeting. You didn't bother to come."

"I couldn't come. Our house was broken into."

"I'm sorry about that." She paused. "You could have phoned."

"I had other things to worry about."

She shrugged. "Well, I must be going. Dr. Long doesn't like to be kept waiting."

She opened the door and then stuck her head back inside. "We should have a staff meeting soon. I have some ideas I'd like to suggest on how to make the store more efficient."

"I bet you have," I said under the jingle of the chimes as she swept away.

That afternoon was unusually busy. I had little patience to deal with the two sales reps who dropped by with catalogues, order forms, posters, bookmarks and gossip. Because a P.D. day had closed the schools, freeing kids to do their Christmas shopping, I had to keep a sharp eye out for shoplifters while at the same time I was inundated with questions and complaints about titles that couldn't be found or had sold out long ago. The sales desk was beside the front door which gave me a view down the length of the shelves and a good look at everyone on their way out. It also meant that I was subjected to icy drafts every time the door was opened.

Dr. Long arrived a few minutes before three o'clock. Average in size, she carried herself with a stern grace that commanded attention. Although in her mid-fifties, her long hair, held back with a jewelled comb, was still a thick glossy black, her face smooth of wrinkles. She wore little make-up. The only times I met her she was dressed in raw silk, beautiful clothes that must have been hand-made to fit her so perfectly.

She came in, bundled up in a black mink coat. On the lapel, a diamond cat winked one green eye.

"How was lunch?" I asked.

"Fine." She never bothered with small talk.

"It's all settled then? Who's to be store manager?"

"Of course. If you agree."

"I think Lil deserves the job. She's been here longest."

"You don't want it?" Dr. Long thumbed through the special order book, noting the number of customers still waiting to receive their Christmas parcels.

"I thought you were offering it to Stephanie."

"I had lunch with Mrs. Thompson," Dr. Long said, "only because she was so insistent. I thought it best to break the news to her alone. I knew she would be disappointed. She's not the type to stay here long. She has ambitions, for one thing, and then the children take up too much of her attention. I need someone I can trust to take care of things for me. You, on the other hand, are quite settled and you don't have any distractions."

"You want me to take the job?"

"But of course. There won't be any changes until Miss Lewis is ready to leave." She looked at her watch. "I'm driving straight back to the city so I don't have time to talk now. We will have a meeting together the next time I come, after Christmas." She picked up the accounts book I'd placed ready for her on the counter.

"I'm not sure I want the job," I said.

"But of course you do," she answered. "It's perfect for you. There'll be more hours of course, once Miss Lewis is gone. And Mrs. Thompson probably won't stay too long either. It will keep you busy, keep your mind off things."

"What do you mean?"

She fiddled with the buttons on her coat. "I've heard of all your troubles. The fire and theft," she said. She shivered slightly. "Quite upsetting for you. It will be good to have something to look forward to, the raise and the responsibility."

"I guess Stephanie's told you about the Harpers and the break-in." I couldn't keep my voice quite free from anger.

"Stephanie?" She frowned, puzzled. "Oh. Of course. Mrs. Thompson. Yes, she does talk a lot. I must be off. Have a good holiday." She swept out the door.

I stared after her. If Stephanie hadn't been talking to her, who had? I was sure Karen and Lil wouldn't have the gall or the opportunity to gossip with the boss and I wasn't aware of anyone else we knew in common. However, the business did give Dr. Long an interest in this town. Perhaps she kept track of events in the local paper. Although, the thought nagged at the back of my mind, my involvement with the Harpers was never mentioned in stories about the fire, and the break-in was too small to rate a report. One more puzzle to deal with.

I dialled the number of the house where Will was working. Before the phone was answered, a customer came to the desk with a pile of books. She leaned forward as I rang up the total.

"That's a terrible price for paperbacks, isn't it?" she said.

I didn't recognize her as one of our regular customers. She had an interesting collection of children's stories and serious fiction.

"These are British imports," I replied. "They're always pretty expensive."

"I remember when Penguins used to be fifty cents. Do you remember the orange covers?"

"Before my time." I needed two bags for her purchases.

"It wasn't that long ago," she protested. "Of course I am buying books for my grandchildren." She laughed at herself. "Time flies. What a cliché, but so true."

Stephanie slammed into the store. "I hope you're satisfied," she hissed.

The customer picked up her books and change. She smiled uncertainly at us both. "I'd better be going," she said. "Merry Christmas."

"Merry Christmas," I answered. Then, "Calm down, Stephanie. What's your problem?"

"You went behind my back," she accused.

"You mean Dr. Long? She surprised me too."

"Oh sure. You're just full of surprises, aren't you?"

I glared at the girls who were inching towards the door behind Stephanie's back. "Are you planning to pay for those books you've put in that bag?" I demanded.

"What books?" one shot back, but the other dropped the blue Eaton's bag she was carrying and the two ran out the door laughing.

I came out behind the desk, picked up the bag, turned the lock, and switched the sign to "Closed." I took Stephanie by the sleeve and bundled her into the storeroom.

"Listen to me," I said. "There's no plot here, no plan to get you. Dr. Long thinks you're too smart and too ambitious for this job. It's a compliment, don't you see? She made me manager because I'm safe and settled. She doesn't want surprises and she's sure I'll keep working away as I've always done. Because I'm stuck here." I was astounded at the anger in my own voice.

"Do you really think so?" Stephanie fingered the fringe of her shawl.

"You're too good for this job," I replied. "You have all those plans about going to work in Ottawa. You've got the kids to think of. How long do you think you'll stay once the divorce and custody are settled? You don't want to be saddled with a responsibility that will get in your way."

"I guess you're right." She tossed her head. "I wasn't thinking it through. And you will do a good job of course. I mean you've been here forever."

"Not much longer than you," I retorted.

"But you've been quite happy with the way things are. I'm always thinking of improvements," her voice lowered in regret. Then she perked up. "But you're right. Better you than me to have to put up with some of the customers. You're always so patient. And you never seem to mind about Dr. Long's insistence that we keep things going in the same old way. Nothing bothers you, does it?"

"No," I answered. "I just go along."

It was dark by the time I closed up. My head ached and each breath whistled. When I coughed, my chest ached. I had an envelope full of cash in one pocket and my gloves stuffed in the other as I fiddled with the stubborn lock. A hand dropped on my shoulder. I spun round, keys in my fist.

"It's you."

Will grinned somewhat sheepishly. "Sorry. I didn't mean to scare you. With all that's been happening lately, I thought you might like some company on the way to the bank."

The sidewalks were still busy with late shoppers rushing for Christmas bargains. The bank was in the next block but its night deposit was around the corner on a side street lined with government offices and travel agencies that always closed early. I sighed with relief when the flap of the deposit chute clicked shut over the day's takings. Will held my hand as we walked back to where he'd parked.

"The garage fixed the lock on the gas tank," he said. "They can't do a paint job until after the holidays, so I put some rustproof filler where the finish has been burnt off. It looks pretty bad, but it'll save the body from the salt."

As he bent to unlock the door, a long black car pulled away from the curb. It had a telephone aerial on its trunk, and two passengers who stared at us as it drove off. I shivered again.

"Are you all right?" Will asked.

"A cold coming on, I think."

"Lot of flu going around."

"That's all I need, to get sick now in the busiest season." A moment later, I added, "Dr. Long came into the store. She offered me the job."

"Rosie, that's great." Will hugged me.

"Yeah." I burrowed my chin into the warm folds of my scarf.

"You don't sound very excited."

"She didn't even ask me if I wanted to stay on, just took my acceptance for granted."

"You've been there three years, you practically run the store as it is now. What more do you want?"

"She says Stephanie has too much ambition to stay here."

"That's Stephanie's fault for carrying on about all her great plans for moving to Ottawa once the divorce is finalized."

"How do you know that?"

"Karen told me. And Stephanie's been complaining to Dr. Long about working on Saturdays with the kids at home. She thought you and Karen, being childless, should do all the Saturday shifts. Apparently she kept saying how things would be different once she gets away from here and back to a real job."

"She always talks too much."

"So what are you going to do?"

"Think about it."

Will started the car. "It seems to me that this might be just what you need. More hours, more pay, a lot more responsibility. You can set the tone for the whole store, get rid of those romances you're always complaining about."

"The good doctor doesn't like changes, as Stephanie reminded me. She'll want things to carry on as they always have been. And it's still not my store."

"So you get all the fun and none of the hassle."

"It's not the same. You of all people should know that."

"Is there something else you'd rather do?"

That silenced me. I gnawed at a nail that had broken earlier when I was unpacking books. The job was murder on my hands.

"We can't afford to buy into another business," Will went on. "Not yet anyway. Wait a couple of years, though, and you can set up a store of your own. With the experience you'll have running the Pocket Book, no bank could refuse you a loan."

"All I do is wait," I grumbled. "My whole life is in suspense. I'm getting pretty sick of it."

"You could look for another job."

"Oh sure. In this town, with the way the economy's going lately? We're lucky that you're still getting work."

"True. That reminds me, I'm almost finished with the Martins. I should have a bit more time free to help you fix up the bedroom."

"There's something else bothering me," I said. "Dr. Long said she knew about all my troubles. How could she have heard about the break-in and the car fire? Neither was reported anywhere."

Will fidgeted. "Maybe she just meant finding the body and the death of the Harpers."

"My dinner with them didn't make the papers either. It's odd. She seemed to imply she knew a lot more about me than she should. I mean, how could she be sure I wouldn't take the job and then get pregnant? I've never told her about that problem. Karen is the only one outside of us who knows the details, and she wouldn't gossip about it. I know she wouldn't."

"She's a gynecologist, isn't she?" Will countered. "Maybe she's been working with the fertility clinic in Toronto, and saw your name there on some files."

"Why would you think that?" I asked, surprised. The idea had never occurred to me. "I thought that kind of information was confidential."

He shrugged. "Seems logical. She could have been looking for someone else and noticed your name. You work for her, so your name would stand out."

"That's pretty far-fetched. More likely Karen or Lil said something. That makes me furious. My private business is private and no one has the right to discuss it behind my back."

"Calm down, Rosie," Will said. "Dr. Long could have

meant almost anything. You may be mistaken about her motives for asking you. I'm sure she thinks you're the best one qualified for the job. You're so touchy these days."

I stared out the window.

After a long silence, Will went back to the earlier topic, "What about going back to school then?"

"What for? And where? I can't bear the thought of commuting to the city." My breath fogged the pane. I drew a series of x's and o's, then erased them with one swipe of my fist.

"Then you should be glad that you've been given the chance to run the store. I think it's just what you need."

"I guess." I sighed. Why wasn't I happier about the new job? Dr. Long's remark about my reliability rankled. What she really meant was that she knew I had no options. I hated this feeling that circumstance was stranding me in a dead-end job.

"Better you than Stephanie," Will chuckled suddenly. "I can't see you staying on there if she had been made manager."

"It would have given me an excuse to leave."

"And do what?"

Again, I had no answer. I changed the subject instead. "I went to the Dunstables after all this morning." There was no point in aggravating Will by repeating the boy's partial admittance of guilt about the car fire, so I described the house, Matty's rude belligerence, and his mother's bruise.

"You think the Reverend hit her?"

"Not him. Matty."

"But she's his mother!"

"More like his slave. They didn't tell me a thing. They don't seem to know where the Reverend is either. Do you think he's taken off?"

"Have they reported him missing to the police?"

"I doubt it. Matty didn't seem too worried about it, and his mother would do whatever he told her. He won't want the police around any more than necessary."

Will made supper when we got home while I soaked in a hot bath. We settled down with books after the dishes were put away, Will with a new publication on interprovincial politics, me with a serial murder. Barely half an hour later, he slammed his book shut.

"I can't stop thinking about what that boy did to our car. Let's go visit the Dunstables again. Maybe the Reverend will be back by now, with some answers for us."

Will parked right in front of the Dunstable house. The drapes, still tightly closed, glowed with light.

"I'll go by myself to the door," I said. "If Mrs. Dunstable is alone, she's more likely to talk to me then to the two of us together. If the Reverend's back, I'll signal."

This time, my knock was answered immediately. Mrs. Dunstable wore the same apron over a plain gray dress. When she saw who was standing there, she tried to close the door. I wedged myself into the opening.

"Is Mr. Dunstable back yet?" I asked.

She stepped back, shaking her head. I squeezed myself in, letting the screen door shut, but holding the inner one open so that Will could clearly see us. The house was very quiet. I glanced involuntarily up the stairs.

"Matthew's not here," she said harshly. "He's gone. Thanks to you." Her lips thinned over her teeth.

"When did he leave?"

"A while ago. Someone phoned for him after you left. Now he's gone. Ian's gone. I'm by myself now." She kneaded her hands together in the skirt of the apron.

"What was your husband's business with Jennifer Rumble?" I got right to the point, afraid that she would begin to cry and refuse to speak. For a moment, I thought she wouldn't answer or would tell me to leave.

Instead, she sat down heavily on one of the lower stairs.

"It was church business. None of my business. Or yours."

"Someone's after me, Mrs. Dunstable. It is my business."

"You think it's Matthew. I know you do. Do you have children?"

"No."

"You," she said. "You're just like that woman. She didn't have a baby of her own, so she tried to take mine. After she came, he started getting into trouble. It was her fault. All her fault."

"The police said he was well-known to them as a trouble-maker."

"The police! What do they know? And how dare you blame my boy for attacking you! You know what he was doing over at that house: dealing drugs. I found envelopes with crystals in them in his room. I knew what they were, I've seen them on TV. He laughed at me, until I flushed them away. Oh, he was angry then." She touched her bruised cheek. "He knows his mother knows what's best for him. He'll come to his senses, now that woman's gone."

"How did you meet her in the first place?"

"She said we could save the babies if we gave her money."

"What babies?"

"The refugees," she said impatiently, "from the death squads. She knew a way to bring orphans into this country. Ian didn't want to get involved because some of the brethren said it wasn't right or legal. I told him we had no choice, we had to save the children. We used the money in the chapel building fund."

"You stole money from your church?"

"Borrowed," she said firmly. "It was for a holy purpose."

"A holy purpose?" I repeated.

"Suffer little children," she said. "When the babies were here, we would be forgiven for not asking permission. Everyone would agree that it was God's will that led us to use the money. Better to save the little ones, than to build a palace of worship."

"So where are the babies?"

"I don't know," she wailed. "The Harpers were supposed to bring me my daughter. Ian went to Toronto to see them and when he came back, he was frightened. He wouldn't talk to me. He blames me for getting us involved with them. And now he's gone and Matthew is gone and my little daughter is lost." She stifled a sob.

She was telling me too much, spilling it out in confessional anguish. I felt so sorry for her, deserted as she was by both her husband and her son. I probably should have left her alone, but the story she was so eager to tell was too intriguing.

"Was Ms. Rumble Matty's lawyer? Is that how you met her?"

"No, the doctor sent her." She rubbed her eyes with the corner of the apron. "I went to see a doctor in Toronto. I lied to Ian. I told him I was going to visit my mother, but I didn't. I went to one of those clinics instead."

"Are you ill? I'm sorry." Guilt at badgering a sick woman fought with my curiousity.

Mrs. Dunstable gave me no chance to leave. She spoke in a whispered monotone I had to strain to hear. "She said they'd have to do tests on Ian too. But when I told him that, he said it was devil's work, that if God meant us to have just one baby, then that's all we would have, that he would not submit his body or mine to science. I think he was afraid, don't you? I think he knew that he was the impotent one." She swallowed a giggle.

"What was the doctor's name? What clinic did you go to?"

"Why? Why do you care? Why do you want to know?"

"It's the same with me," I said. "I can't have babies either."

She leaned close and grasped my arm. Nails as long and curved as talons dug into my flesh. "Cursed," she hissed. "We are daughters of Eve and cursed. But I found the way to get me my daughter and no one can take her from me."

"The doctor?" I tried again. "Was it Dr. Long by any chance?"

She dropped my arm. "If you know, why do you ask? Do you know where the children are?" she demanded, her voice raw. "Do you know what they did with the children?"

"Mrs. Dunstable, I need you to come with me, to tell what you know to Constable Finlay. He's a detective, a good man. He'll help you. I know he will."

"No police," she said. "I won't go. If you bring one of them here, I won't talk to him. I won't get Ian into any more trouble. He did what he did for me. I'll deny I told you anything."

"But you need some help," I said. "And I do too. There's someone out there who wants to hurt me. He thinks I met Jennifer Rumble and that I know all her secrets. If he suspects what you know, he may come after you too."

"I don't need any help. Except to find my baby. Look," she said, pulling a small square of paper out of her pocket. "Here's the picture they gave me of my little girl. Isn't she beautiful?"

The photograph was a black-and-white close-up print of a very small baby. Her mouth was open in a toothless smile, her eyes big and black in a round face framed by a knit hat that hugged her ears. One small fist curled up towards her chin.

"She's very sweet," I said.

Mrs. Dunstable snatched the picture back, kissed it and held it to her breasts. She rocked back and forth, the step creaking under her weight. Her eyes were closed, her lips moving as if in prayer.

"Mrs. Dunstable, listen to me," I pleaded.

She refused to open her eyes and look at me. Her whole face was squeezed tight in denial.

"Why did your husband come to see me?" I asked. "Why did Matty set fire to my car? Why did they think I had anything to do with all this?"

"Matty didn't touch your car," she snapped, her eyes blazing green in the gloom of the hall. "Don't you dare say that."

"All right, all right. Take it easy."

"When Ian told me he saw Simon Harper in your store, we thought you might be working with them too. The baby was supposed to be here a month ago! No one would tell us where she is. Rumble was dead and Harper said he would reveal where the money came from if we didn't stop bothering them. Ian was at his wit's end."

"Where is Mr. Dunstable now?" I asked.

Outside, a car horn beeped. I held up my hand to show Will I'd heard and that I was all right, needing just a few more minutes to get the whole story.

Tears continued to streak down her face. She sniffed them back. When she spoke, she spoke to the picture, not to me. "He went to see Mr. Whitman. Mr. Whitman said you were at the Harper's house when it burned down."

"Mr. Whitman?" Here was a new name to add to the puzzle.

"They were meeting at the new church. I heard Matthew tell you that." She loomed over me from her perch on the stairs, spitting her questions right into my face. "What do you want from me? Why do you keep asking me these things? Why do you keep knocking on my door? Why don't you mind your own business and leave me alone?"

I opened the screen and stepped out on to the porch. "I'll go now," I said. "I'm sorry for disturbing you. Please believe me, I have nothing to do with any of this. I don't know anything about drugs or babies. Honestly."

She simply stared at me with those cold green eyes.

"I'm so sorry," I said again, helpless to give her any other kind of comfort.

She slammed the door behind me. I walked quickly to the curb. Will pushed the door open and I slipped in.

"What a scene," I sighed.

"You were in there long enough. Did you find out where Dunstable is?"

"Out at the new church on the highway. He was supposed

to be meeting a Mr. Whitman there."

"Who's he?"

"She didn't say. She was so worked up, I'm amazed she told me as much as she did. I feel so sorry for her. Matty's taken off, and the Reverend hasn't come home."

"You think she'll be all right?" Will nosed the car into the street.

"I hope so. I can't go back there again, though. Maybe we should try to find someone who belongs to their church who can stay with her for awhile."

"Maybe we should go out to the church and see if we can find Dunstable for her."

"All right."

Will turned the car away from the river and headed back through town towards the highway. The main streets had been ploughed bare of snow. Sand and salt hissed under the tires.

I fiddled with the radio dial, trying to tune in the classical music station. Its low wattage made reception erratic at best. "By the way, you're not going to believe what she told me about Dr. Long."

Will stopped the car, none too gently, as a yellow light switched to red. "Dr. Long? What has she got to do with this?"

"Apparently, the Dunstables were having trouble conceiving a second baby. Though God knows why they would want another one, given their charming son. Anyway, Mrs. Dunstable went to see Dr. Long at a fertility clinic in Toronto. After her visit there, Jennifer Rumble got in touch to suggest they adopt a baby through her, a baby they would be able to save from death squads by paying a lot of money for it. They stole money from the church, and gave it to Rumble who told them the Harpers would deliver the child. They never did."

"Do you think she made it all up?" Will asked.

"It gets crazier. She says that Rumble was a bad influence on Matty; that it was Rumble who got him into dealing dope."

"She sounds completely mad."

"Wouldn't you be if your son was a drugged-out delinquent and your husband had disappeared? She was so upset. I didn't know whether to keep asking her questions or not, but she seemed to want to talk. It just doesn't make any sense. Especially Dr. Long's involvement. I can't believe it."

"Drugs and baby buyers. Not exactly what you'd expect from small town fundamentalists, is it?"

"None of this is what you'd expect to happen in a small town."

"Here's the church." Will turned the car off the highway.

The Clear Light Mission was a fundamentalist sect which began holding meetings in an abandoned schoolhouse, then graduated to a small church whose own established congregation had withered away. As Dunstable's preaching drew in larger crowds, they organized fundraising events to build a new chapel on the outskirts of town. They even held an old-fashioned roof-raising party to publicize its construction. The newspaper photograph showed Dunstable in his black coat, one finger pointing to the sky as an army of shirt-sleeved men swarmed over the beams and uprights while a flock of women wearing flowered aprons tended barbecues and long trestle tables. Children ran about. I thought of Matty and the vanity of nostalgia.

The front of the church faced a wide white lawn neatly bisected by narrow shovelled paths. Parking space for several hundred cars had been cleared on the other three sides of the imposing brick edifice which was built in the shape of a cross, the long lateral section two storeys high to accommodate offices and schoolrooms. The building was dark and deserted.

"It doesn't look like anyone's here," Will said.

"We may as well take a look around."

It was bitterly cold outside. As the wind blew clouds across the full moon, shadows raced across the snow. I rattled the padlocked chain which looped through the handles of the side door near which Will had parked.

"Mr. Dunstable," I called. "Are you in there?"

Will wandered around the back. "There's a car parked here," he shouted.

It was the small black sedan I'd last seen idling outside our house on the day of the Reverend's visit. It was lightly dusted with snow, the windows opaque with frost. A hose twisted up from the tailpipe and in through the window which had been stuffed with a tartan scarf. Will tried the doors but they were all locked. He scratched at the ice on the windshield.

"Oh no." He pulled at the door handle. It didn't budge. "There's someone in there."

"Dunstable?"

We stared at each other over the hood of the car. A string of tractor trailers rattled by on the highway. In their wake, a car turned into the parking lot, its tires suddenly silent as it wheeled on to the hard packed snow. The engine roar slowed down to a purr. A door slammed.

"Let's get out of here." Will raced around the corner.

From the safety of the shadow formed by the deep angle of the cross, we could see the long, black car of my nightmares. The driver leaned on the hood, the smoke of a cigarette making a halo around his head. Another man stood at the front door, his ear pressed to the glass panel.

Will touched my arm. I looked at him and he motioned for me to keep quiet and to follow. We ran back to our car which was hidden from the newcomers on the other side of the church.

"Do you think they're police?" he asked, when we had eased the doors shut.

"Not likely. Not in that car."

"Hold on, then. I'll race around past them, and get out on the highway before they have a chance to turn around."

"No, there's a better way." I thought hard for a moment. "I remember when all the fuss was made at council about permission to build here, about access to the highway and fears about traffic congestion and a fire route. They had to agree to put in a back entrance."

"Someone's coming." Will said. He switched on the engine. Its roar drowned a sudden shout. A man was running towards us, one hand outstretched. I feared that it held a gun.

"Follow that ploughed track," I cried. "It's got to lead to the back exit."

Tires spat snow as Will shoved the car into gear. We bounced over ruts, the black wall of trees along the bush line looming closer. Behind us came headlights. With one hand, I buckled on my seatbelt while the other clutched the dash for balance.

"There." I pointed to a small cut which showed in the snow banked along the fenced property line.

Will swerved into it. The car lurched over one drift, two, then squealed onto bare pavement. In seconds, we were out on the highway, heading back towards the safety of town.

TWELVE

Will headed straight for the mall, the busiest place in town at this hour of the evening. After the chill outdoors, the mall seemed stuffy and overheated; we elbowed our way through the throng to the hotel entrance at the far end of the rows of shops.

The hotel had two bars; we chose the upstairs room where salespeople on expense accounts sipped malt whiskey and tried to pick each other up. The walls were lined with mirrors in which candleflame flickered. We slipped into a banquette at the far end near an exit. A large woman in heavy make-up leaned confidentially over the keyboard of a grand piano and crooned into a microphone. The words of her song melted into the chatter of voices, the tinkle of keys, the rhythmic pulse of the drum machine, and the click of ice on glass.

I hadn't even had time to unbutton my coat when the waitress appeared, balancing an empty tray on her hip.

"Scotch?" Will asked me.

I nodded, and he gave the order. "Two, Johnny Walkers. Ice, no water."

It was hard to see faces in the dim light. I recognized no one, and no one followed us in. As soon as the waitress walked off, pocketing her tip, I asked Will, "Should we call Finlay?"

"What's the use?" He stirred his drink with a purple plastic sword. "The cops don't seem to be doing anything about this case."

"What about Dunstable?"

"Someone will find him soon enough. His car is not exactly hidden. We've done enough finding of bodies to report yet another one."

"Poor Mrs. Dunstable." I sipped my drink and pulled a face. The first hit of hard liquor always caught in my throat; the second went down a lot easier. "Do you remember me talking about Cindy Reed, the girl who lives in the apartment above Karen?"

"What about her?"

"Her boyfriend is the one who saved our car the other night. When the cops caught Matty Dunstable, he seemed to recognize him. Maybe we should go over there and talk to them some more. Maybe he knows where Matty is."

"What good will finding the boy do?"

"Maybe we could persuade him to go home. His mother will really need him now. She shouldn't be alone when she gets the news. And maybe you can talk some sense into him, convince him to leave us alone."

"You do think he had something to do with the break-in then?"

"Oh yes. I knew that as soon as I met him the other day. He's a real punk, just the kind to destroy for destruction's sake. I bet all our stuff's up in his room right now."

"Good evening, Will. And you must be Mrs. Cairns," a loud voice interrupted. The speaker leaned heavily against our table, both hands clutching at the rim to help her keep her balance.

"Kirsten. Carl." Will stood up to shake hands and introduced the couple standing there to me. "My wife, Rosalie. This is Kirsten Loring and her husband, Carl."

Although the woman was short, her body bulky under a red wool coat, the man with her was even shorter and stockier. They looked like twins, her hair cropped close to her skull, his head almost bald. Where he was pale as if he spent too much time indoors, reading, her face was flushed, her eyes bright in their rings of shadows.

"Will you join us?" I tried to make my welcome as unfriendly as possible, but a client was a client. It paid to be polite.

Kirsten bit her lip and glanced at her husband.

"Thank you, but no," he said. "We must be going."

"All ready for your baby?" Will asked. He perched between table and chair, one hand resting on its back to steady himself. His smile wavered.

"She's not coming. The adoption's been called off." Kirsten's voice was loud and bitter. "We're not getting our baby after all."

The waitress appeared with her tray.

"Bring me another drink," Kirsten ordered.

The waitress looked at Will, who nodded. She checked the pad on her tray. "Vodka, wasn't it? And a pint of lager?"

"None for me," Carl shook his head. "I'm driving."

Kirsten plumped down in a chair beside me. Carl pulled over another chair and the two men sat. The drinks arrived. Kirsten downed hers in one long convulsive swallow.

"Cheers," she muttered.

"I'm sorry," Carl said. "We shouldn't stay. We were told just two days ago that the baby wasn't coming, after all this time. We thought maybe coming out, being surrounded by other people, would make it easier to bear, but now we must go home. Put the crib away. Start all over again. Somehow."

Kirsten caught back a sob. She grabbed the tissue I offered and savagely wiped her face. "That bastard," she hissed. "We gave him money to find the baby for us and then he comes to us and says we can't have her and the money's gone."

"It's not the money," Carl protested.

"I know." Kirsten's face screwed up again. "I'm sorry, Will, Rosalie. But I want that baby so badly. We even have a picture of her. Look." She began to scramble in her purse, a large leather bag that dangled from a wide shoulder strap.

Carl clicked his tongue. "I thought you threw that picture

out yesterday."

She looked at him in horror. "She's my baby." She smoothed the shiny surface of the photograph with one finger, then thrust it at us.

I stared at the photograph of a smiling baby, the same photograph and the same baby that Mrs. Dunstable so treasured. "How did you find her?" I asked.

Will grimaced and Carl sighed. Will gave me a look that clearly asked why I was encouraging her when she was obviously in no shape to talk.

She leaned against my shoulder and traced the outlines of the baby's face with one trembling finger.

"We went first to the Children's Aid, then to other government agencies. They all said we were too old, us! They said the waiting list was too long even for older children. But we wanted a little baby who would know only us as her parents."

"We both wanted a girl," Carl added.

"Yes. It was magic how we found her, as if it was meant to be. My community awareness class was discussing the kind of activities their churches were involved in, those that go to church. One of them told me about this program for helping refugees in Central America. He told me in confidence that they sometimes arranged adoptions too." She swallowed, set down her glass.

"I think it's time to go." Carl pushed back his chair.

Kirsten shrugged out of her coat and raised her glass. "I want another drink," she announced. "We came out to see people. So, now we see people."

The waitress deposited another tall glass and took the empty one away. Kirsten sucked the stalk of celery that stood upright in the thick red drink, then used it to push the ice cubes under over and over again.

"I went to see the preacher," she continued. "One of these hellfire and brimstone types, but a decent man. I thought. He said the church had nothing to do with it."

Carl took up the story. "We think he must have passed on news of our interest. A lawyer from Toronto came to see us. He told us that there was such a program for private adoptions, a humanitarian service to save babies from the civil war. It was all secret, a matter of immigration regulations and security, getting the babies out of the guerilla camps in the highlands."

"A man?" I interrupted. "The lawyer was a man?"

Carl looked at me curiously. "Yes."

"Go on." Will was hooked on the story now. "What happened?"

"It cost a lot of money, but we didn't care. He said he would make all the arrangements for us. He gave us this picture just two months ago. Her name is Eugenie; she's five months old tomorrow. Her mother was killed by government troops and the baby is in an orphanage. It's run by nuns, but they have little money and the conditions are very uncertain. We were supposed to be able to bring her home for Christmas."

"Was it Matty Dunstable who told you about the adoption?"

"How did you know?" Kirsten stared at me. "He's one of my favourite students. Mixed up, but a good boy at heart. He really cared when I told him how much I wanted a baby."

"His father came to see us two days ago," Carl added. "He was the one who told us the adoption was off."

"I'd like to kill that man," Kirsten spat. "We went to his house to see him, to get an explanation, but he wouldn't talk to us. His wife slammed the door in our faces."

"When did you go there?" Will asked.

"Last night, late," Kirsten answered. "After dinner, between nine and ten o'clock. He'd come the day before to say that there'd been some trouble at the other end, that the baby wouldn't be released after all since the mother had been found. Such a hypocrite in his black clothes, so serious and sad. I said to him, what about the lawyer, what does he have to say about this. He said the lawyer had disappeared with all our money. I don't believe him. He's in it up to his neck, and he'll pay for it."

Her voice rang out. Faces turned in our direction. The piano player faltered, then began to sing "Moon River." The waitress left the bar and hurried over to our table. Carl put his arm around his wife.

"We are just leaving," he said to the room at large. He shook his head at us. "It was very cruel, very cruel. He stood at the door, wouldn't even come in. Just gave us this bad news and left. We didn't think until later to ask about the money, and now we can't find him, and no one answers the phone in the lawyer's office."

"I think we should go to the police," Kirsten said. "They took our money, and gave nothing back. That is illegal."

"I think getting the baby this way is not entirely legal," Carl shook his head. "Stupid anyway. We wanted the child so much, we never thought about the rights of the matter. We thought we were doing good, saving her. You can understand?"

"Oh yes." I cradled Kirsten's hand in mine. "I think you should wait until you're a bit calmer before you talk to the police."

"Yes." Carl agreed. "Let's go home and try to get some sleep."

They stood up again, awkward in their heavy coats.

"One more thing," I asked. "What was the lawyer's name?"

"Lawyer?" Kirsten shook her head, clearing it. "Whitman, I think. Like the poet."

"Did you ever meet anyone else connected with the scheme? The Harpers? Jennifer Rumble?"

"Isn't she the woman you found in the river?" Kirsten gasped.

"We must go," Carl insisted, dragging at his wife's arm.

She turned pale, her hand to her mouth, staring at me through eyes blurry with unshed tears. Then she fled towards the exit, stumbling against chairs in her haste to get outdoors. Carl shrugged apologetically, and followed.

"Poor woman," Will murmured, staring after them.

"How could they be so stupid as to get involved in such a shady operation?" I drained my glass.

"I can understand it, wanting a baby so badly you'd do almost anything to get one. Some people are like that, Rosie."

"Not me," I said. I put on my coat. "Let's go to Karen's right away. Gary works late most nights at the gas station, I seem to remember. He'll just be getting home about now. Maybe with you there, he'll talk. It's time we got to the bottom of all this."

Karen met us at the top of the stairs. "Cindy's at my place," she whispered. "I thought I should warn you, she's in rough shape."

The girl lay curled up on the futon, her head buried in the crook of her arms. She wore a pink track suit, her blonde hair pulled back into a loose pony tail that hung limp over one shoulder. She looked up when we came in, her face streaked with tears, her eyes red and swollen. She unwound to her feet, rocking as though the slightest noise would knock her over.

"I've got to be going," she whispered.

Karen put her arm around her shoulders. "You can stay, Cindy. You know Rosie and this is her husband, Will. They're good friends of mine."

Cindy shook her head. "I'll be okay, now. Thanks, Karen, for being here for me." They hugged briefly. Cindy caught back a sob, then straightened and crossed to the door. "See you," she said and was gone.

"What was that all about?" Will asked. He plumped down on the pile of pillows, wiggling and shifting them into a comfortable shape.

"We've come to talk to Gary. Is he home?"

"Gary's left her. He came back early from work today to tell her he was through. Packed his bags and was about to go when that boy arrived. Matty Dunstable. Waltzed into their apartment and picked up Gary's suitcase. Seems he was going too. With Gary. As a couple."

"You're joking." I sank down on the futon. "We wanted to talk to Gary about Matty. We thought they might know each other. I didn't realize they were such close friends."

"No one did. At least Cindy had no clue. She took Gary in when he got evicted from his last place, gave up her job to help him out with his uncle's business, and then, he knocks her up and walks out on her with his boyfriend."

"She's pregnant?"

"Four months. Too late to do anything about it. She thought they were going to get married. I guess he had other plans."

"Didn't she have any idea about Matty?"

"Just saw him that one time on the stairs and then the night he fire-bombed your car. She's so innocent."

"Dumb, you mean," Will muttered.

"That's not fair." Karen turned on him. She was tense with anger and concern for the girl. "She trusted the guy. He'd made a few mistakes, but he swore he was going straight. And he never beat her or treated her badly. Until now."

"Sorry," said Will. "I just think she should have realized that a guy with his record might not be too dependable."

"What do you know about him? Or her, for that matter? Who do you think you are to judge their lives?"

The kettle whistled.

"Shall I get coffee?" I tried to ease the strain. "Can we be friends again?"

"I'll get it," Karen said. She stalked to the door. With one hand pulling back the beaded curtain, she turned and smiled weakly. "Now it's my turn to be sorry, Will. I shouldn't have yelled at you like that. It's just that things finally seemed to be going right for Cindy. And then this has to happen. It's not fair."

"Pax?" Will asked.

"Pax." She disappeared into the kitchen, returning after a long pause carrying a tray laden with a carafe, thick blue pottery mugs and a matching sugar bowl. We busied ourselves pouring coffee. I thought it safe to return to the matter that brought us here. "Did you see Matty before they left?"

Karen nodded.

"Did he look upset? Or worried?"

Karen was puzzled. "He seemed to be enjoying himself from what I could tell. I came out in the hall when I heard Cindy screaming upstairs. Matty was on his way out with a suitcase, a big grin on his face. I tried to stop Gary to ask him what was going on, but he just rushed by. I'll say this for him, he looked none too proud of himself."

"I should think so," Will said. "What kind of creep is he, anyway? Sorry, Karen, but I think he has a lot of grief to answer for."

"Oh, Cindy won't say anything against him. Yet. She's blaming Matty. Apparently he hooked up with Gary not too long ago and they've been involved in some kind of business. She said she should have got suspicious when Gary bought that truck of his for cash. But she's just a kid, not even eighteen. She thought he'd take care of her."

"What's she going to do now?"

"Who knows?"

We sipped our drinks in silence, hands cupping the warm mugs.

"Why did you want to see Matty anyway?" Karen asked.

"We wanted to ask him some questions about the Reverend." I didn't want to involve Karen in this any more than necessary, so said nothing about our discovery in the church parking lot, our conversation with the Lorings, or Dr. Long's possible involvement in some kind of baby buying ring.

She looked closely at me, her eyes narrowed. "What's the secret?" she demanded.

"What secret?" I tried to laugh.

"You two are hopeless at mysteries. I know you're keeping something from me. What's going on?"

"I got the manager's job," I said.

"I know that already. Lil told me. She's happy for you, and so am I. But that's not what you wanted to see Matty Dunstable about."

Before I could think of a possible answer, a voice shouted, "Police," and a sharp rapping shook the door. We looked at each other in surprise. Will shrugged. Karen grimaced, put her cup down on the tray and went to answer the summons.

The young constable standing there was a stranger to all of us. At this rate, I thought to myself, we'll soon know the entire police force. There can't be that many left we haven't met.

"William Cairns? Rosalie Cairns?"

We nodded.

"Please come down to the station with me. You can take your own car," he added. "I'll follow you."

"What's the matter?" Will asked. "What do you need us for this time?"

The policeman shrugged. "Constable Finlay wants to talk to you. That's all I know."

At the station, a uniformed woman behind the front desk murmured our names into a telephone. She nodded to us and pushed a button on the console in front of her. A grilled door swung open. The young constable, still silent on why we were there, led us up some broad carpeted stairs to a series of offices on the second floor. It looked much like any professional building, one wide room with orderly rows of desks, separated by moveable dividers of padded orange cloth, and each crowded with a computer monitor and keyboard, a telephone, and orderly stacks of files. Doors along the side opposite to the windows led to private offices and what I assumed might be interrogation rooms.

A group gathered in one cubicle broke apart as we entered. Finlay was leaning back in his chair, his feet up on the desktop and resting on a green folder. He waved a large cigar in our direction and slowly sat up. The others drifted off. I recognized Olan and McPhail.

"So here you are." Finlay stubbed out his cigar with a flourish. He smiled, a little sheepishly. "Gift from the guys," he explained. "My wife's just had a baby, a boy, nine pounds, six ounces."

"Congratulations," Will muttered sourly. He looked around for a chair.

"It's why you haven't been able to reach me. I've been on paternity leave."

"Is it your first?" I asked.

"Nope. Fourth. Two pair. Here, Maggie, send us a chair over, will you?" he called.

McPhail was standing by a coffee machine. She turned and shoved a wheeled chair in our direction. Will caught it as it hurtled by, and held it for me. I sat down and he leaned against the back-rest, brooding over me.

"How's your dog?" Finlay asked.

"She's all right now. A little wobbly sometimes, but full of beans." Perhaps if I kept chattering, I thought, we might get through this meeting without any difficult questions.

Will wasn't so sanguine. "You didn't have us brought here to discuss Sadie's health, did you?"

"No, no, quite the contrary." Finlay leaned forward, his eyes shifting from me to Will and back. "What do you know about Ian Dunstable?"

Will's hand gripped my shoulder.

"He comes into the store," I answered.

"You visited his wife, I understand. Twice. Or should I say, his widow."

"You've found him?" I couldn't keep the relief from my voice.

"You knew he was missing, did you?"

"We don't have to answer your questions," Will broke in.

"Afraid of something, Mr. Cairns?"

"Not from you."

The two men glared at each other.

Finlay turned back to me." His car was found parked behind that church they have out on the highway. He was inside, sucking on the exhaust pipe. Looks like suicide."

"Looks like?" Will queried at the same moment that I was asking, "Was there a note?"

"No." Finlay tapped the file. He inched it in my direction. "We found this. It's some kind of ledger, initials, figures that probably refer to money. A lot of money. You know anything about this?"

We both shook our heads.

"It's not his handwriting, though," Finlay continued. "His wife confirmed that. We think it might be Jennifer Rumble's."

"The missing file," I breathed, relieved. "The one that the Harpers and the man in the park are after. Dunstable had it all along. But then why . . ."

"Why what?" Finlay snapped.

"Nothing," I said. I remembered how anxious Dunstable had seemed that day he came to our house. Why would he be so worried about the ledger when apparently he already had it? "I'm just glad you've got it. That is her journal, isn't it? The one the others want?"

"Could be," he nodded. He turned to Will. "When you were working in Immigration, did you ever run into Simon Harper or his wife?"

"No. I never heard of them before they came into the store and asked Rosie out to their place. She never talked about him and neither did Jennifer Rumble the very few times I met her."

"Yes, a bit odd, don't you think? You all knowing each other without knowing each other, so to speak." He paused. "I still don't understand why you didn't tell us right away that you knew Ms. Rumble."

Will straightened up, his hand still on my shoulder. "We've been over and over this. How many times do I have to tell you, I hardly knew the woman. Why do you keep bringing it up?"

"You knew about their relationship?" Finlay turned to me.

"It wasn't a relationship." Will shouted. "It was business."

"Will says he hadn't seen her for years," I spoke quietly. "He wouldn't lie to me about it."

"But you knew about her then?"

"Knew about what?" Will interrupted. "You make it sound as if we were having an affair or something."

"Weren't you?"

"No."

Finlay pursed his lips. The fluorescent lights in the ceiling fixtures flickered and hummed. I felt sick, as if the drinks we'd had in the bar and the coffee we'd barely drunk at Karen's were warring with each other. I was sweating and shivering at the same time. Will squeezed my shoulder. I shrugged his hand away.

He sighed. "Once again, for the record. I did know Jennifer Rumble for a brief period about six years ago, maybe a month of business meetings in all. Once we bumped into each other in the subway and went for coffee. She had just left a Bay Street firm, where she'd been only one of a battalion of lawyers, and was just starting out on her own with one partner. She never mentioned his name or, for that matter, whether her partner was a man or a woman. We talked about working for oneself, about having a dream and realizing it."

He turned the chair around so I had to face him. "You know how I hated that job, how I felt I couldn't keep working in that office any longer. You were so wrapped up in your own misery. After your mother died and you went back to the library, all I ever heard about was how much you hated working there. You didn't want to listen to me. I was afraid to leave and afraid to stay. I was worried about committing all our savings to my own dream. What if it failed? Jennifer was a shoulder for me to cry on. She understood. That's all. I swear it to you, Rosie."

"That's all very well," Finlay broke in. "Perhaps you can explain why your initials and home phone number are in this file, then?"

I stood up abruptly, sending the chair rolling back towards another desk. It hit with a clang that drew heads up, facing our way.

"I've had enough. I want to go home."

Finlay shrugged. "The message was, you wanted to see me."

"I guess we made a mistake." I started for the door.

After a moment, Will came after me. I had pulled it open before Finlay spoke again.

"I'd stay away from Mrs. Dunstable if I were you," he drawled. "She's none too happy about your little visit. And I'd stop playing detective too. Someone might get hurt."

I slammed the door behind me.

THIRTEEN

"Look, Rosie," Will said miserably. "There wasn't anything serious between Jennifer Rumble and me. You've got to believe it."

I rolled over, pulling the pillow over my head to block out the light he had left burning. We'd driven home in silence. Sadie had been sleeping so heavily, drugged with the pills the vet had prescribed for her, that she didn't wake when we came in the door. Will had to carry her outside for her evening walk. One of us would have to take her back to the vet's in the morning. One more worry to keep me awake. All I wanted was sleep.

The bedroom was still a mess. Hideous salmon-coloured paint appeared where the wallpaper had been scraped away. Cans of paint and the stepladder filled one corner, waiting for us to find the time to finish fixing up the room. The dressing table and all our clothes were in the study; the bed was too big to move. Still shivering with cold, I put on a long-sleeved nightdress and crawled under the new duvet.

"I don't want to talk about it." I muttered.

"We should clear the air."

I sat up, dislodging the blankets. "Clear what up? We promised we'd never keep secrets from each other. You lied to me about Jennifer Rumble from the beginning."

"I didn't know it was her until her name was published. I told you then that I'd met her, but I didn't see any point in talking about a relationship that was no more than a few conversations."

"You should have told me, warned me about it. Imagine how I felt when Diane and Simon kept talking about the two of you, as if I should have known that something was going on."

"You never told me about Simon."

"For heaven's sake, that happened years before I met you, when I was a kid. There was nothing to "us." One kiss. That's all."

"I never even kissed Jennifer."

"This is ridiculous." I thought I might get more sleep downstairs on the sofa.

As I started out of bed, Will caught my arm. "You're not being fair, Rosie. Why are you trying to blame me? I had nothing to do with Jennifer's death. Nothing!"

"That's what you say," I sneered. I pulled my arm away from his grasp, but didn't leave the bed.

"I'm not the villain here," he insisted. "And you're no victim. Finding fault with me is a way for you to get out of confronting what's really bothering you: your boredom with the way your life is going."

"Now you're a psychologist?"

He sighed, and lay back down, one hand over his eyes. "It doesn't take a medical degree to see that you're unhappy. I wish there was something I could do or say to make you feel better. But you won't listen to me."

"I'm listening now."

"I'll go over it again, for the last time. All right?"

"All right."

"You were so upset about finding that body that I didn't want to make things worse for you by talking about her."

"Thanks," I spat. "Is there anything else you thought I'd be better off not knowing?"

"All right," he said. He sat up, his head in his hands. "I did see her again about three months ago. You know the half of it now, anyway, after talking to Mrs. Dunstable. I met Dr. Long one day downtown when she came to do the books. We had coffee, and I told her about our infertility problem."

"How could you? To my boss?"

"She was also a doctor, a specialist in these things. It's been driving me crazy, Rosie, you know that. And you too. If you had a baby everything would be so much better."

"Right," I said. "Let's take an easy way out."

"Let me tell you the story, okay?"

I lay back down, pulling the duvet up to my nose. I knew I wasn't going to like what I was about to hear, but I was tired of secrets and confusion.

Will lay down beside me. He didn't look at me, but addressed one long crack that snaked up the wall and across the ceiling to the overhead light. "Dr. Long was very sympathetic. She said she couldn't help you if you weren't ready to help yourself. About a week later, I got a call from Jennifer. She wanted to meet me to talk about adoption."

"And did you?"

"No. I knew how you felt about that."

"You wanted to see her though."

"I wanted a child, damn it." He banged one fist on the mattress. "I wanted a child. I want you. You come first. I didn't do anything about her call."

"So why have you kept this from me?"

"I told Finlay ages ago, when he came to see us at the house. You remember. I asked him not to tell you, that it would only upset you. I didn't want to worry you."

"Diane Harper said you'd been going out recently with Jennifer. That man said you had dinner with her in a candlelit restaurant."

"They were lying. I had coffee with Dr. Long, but I only spoke to Jennifer on the phone. Maybe they got names mixed up, or saw my phone number in that file and jumped to conclusions. Same as Finlay. He believed me before but now, with Dunstable's death, he's getting desperate to solve this case. But I've never met her since we worked on that case five years ago. I've never talked to her since then except that one time on the phone. I swear this is the truth, Rosie."

I sniffed back the tears that were burning my sinuses. I'd filled the hot water bottle with boiling water and now hugged it to my stomach which ached and cramped. My toes, stretching out, bumped against his foot. I pulled abruptly away.

Will suddenly sat up. "Wait a minute. I've just remembered something."

"What?" I growled.

"Jennifer's lover. She mentioned him years ago when we were talking dreams about the future. She wanted children too, but he wasn't keen." Will clutched my arm. "His name was John. John Whitman."

"The lawyer who contacted both Mrs. Dunstable and the Lorings." I sat up now too.

"He must be here in town."

"I'm sure he's the one who's been following me. I'm going to phone Finlay right now."

I ran into the study, and punched the numbers out on the phone. Finlay took my call right away. He must have been expecting more dramatic news, for when I told him about Whitman, he merely sighed.

"We've known about him from the beginning," he said. "We talked to him along with the Harpers. None of them knew anything about Rumble's death."

"But he's here in town," I insisted.

"Did Mrs. Dunstable say she'd seen him?"

"No, she just said she'd spoken to him. But I saw him, the man in the park who threatened me."

"As far as we know, Whitman is not in the area. Have you met him before? Can you make a positive identification?"

"It's so obvious," I cried. "He used to be Rumble's lover. Diane told me that Jennifer's ex-boyfriend was insanely jealous, and had been threatening them, accusing them of murdering her. She said they had a court order to keep him away from them, and that they'd come to the cottage to get away from him."

"First I've heard about it."

"Maybe Whitman killed Rumble in a jealous rage."

"They came all the way to a strange town to have a lover's quarrel?" Finlay grumbled. "We investigated Whitman and he's got an alibi for the day she died. And he told us that he'd broken off their engagement, that she was the one who wanted the marriage and was distraught when he called it off. He thought maybe that's why she killed herself."

"What about the Harpers? Where was he when their cottage burned down?"

"Probably at home in bed. As they were when their woodstove caught fire. Accident and coincidence, Mrs. Cairns. It happens all the time."

"You can't believe that." I stamped my foot.

"What I believe is my business," he said. His voice softened. "Haven't you had enough trouble, Mrs. Cairns? Why can't you be sensible and let me take care of things? It's my job."

"But that man is out there somewhere and he still thinks I have some secret information. And I don't. And you don't seem to be able to catch him."

"I'm working on it, don't you worry about that. It'll all be over in a day or so. I wish you'd get out of town for awhile. Now, please, keep out of the way, and look after yourself. Good-night." He hung up.

"I'm going to Toronto," I told Will when I came back to bed. I was too upset to tell him everything Finlay had said. The last person to speak like that to me was my mother when I was sixteen and chasing Simon Harper. And that was a very long time ago.

"I've no right to ask you to stay," he said quietly. "I'm sorry I lied to you, but I did so for your sake."

"I believe you. I think." I said. "I'm only going for the day to visit Whitman's office to prove that he is the man who's been following me."

Will groaned. "And if he's innocent? What if you barge into his office and he turns out to be a total stranger?"

I shrugged. "Then I'll have to look for the villain somewhere else."

"You mean me?"

I didn't answer.

Will finally spoke again. "I can't drive down with you tomorrow. The deadline for the Martin kitchen is Friday and I can't lose any more time. Can you wait for the weekend?"

"I'll take the bus."

We both lay awake for a long time in the darkness, the sheets cool in the careful space we kept empty between us.

When the alarm jolted me out of sleep, the room was still dark. I dressed quickly without bothering to turn on the light. Will remained in bed, a lump of silent suffering. I put Sadie in the backyard while I made coffee, drinking it in the kitchen while watching the sky over the hills to the east begin to lighten. The commuter bus left for the city at seven-thirty. By the time a cab delivered me to the station, there was already a line of people waiting: men and women alike clutching briefcases, newspapers, and steaming styrofoam cups from the all-night donut shop across the street.

I'd hoped I could sit alone and have a chance to nap. I boarded as soon as I could and sank into a window seat towards the front, in the *No Smoking* section. The glass was streaked with grime and the green tint meant to cut down on sun glare transformed the empty parking lot into a bleak monochromatic wasteland. There was little conversation, the murmurings of strangers as they lifted their belongings into the overhead racks, took off their coats, and settled down. The driver walked up the aisle, collecting tickets and counting spaces. More people got on. A matronly woman in a thick cloth coat, overweight and over-perfumed, plumped down beside me. Her friend took the aisle seat opposite. Immediately, the two leaned towards each other to continue their gossip. The door clanged shut and the bus roared into gear, lurching out on to the street and heading out of town.

I tapped my seat-mate on the shoulder. When she turned to me, surprised, I nodded across to her friend. "I'll be happy to change seats," I offered.

"How kind." The woman's smile contorted her mouth, the lipstick spread generously over teeth and chin.

She stood up, swaying regally, one white hand on the high, upholstered back of the seat in front while I edged around her. Her friend grabbed my arm for support as she heaved herself up. I nearly lost my balance as the bus made a sharp turn on to the highway south.

"Thank you," she gasped. As soon as the two were settled, their heads bent together and the steady hiss of whispering began.

I sat down in the still-warm seat. My new companion was a balding man, neatly dressed in suit and tie, face buried in the business section of the morning paper. He didn't acknowledge the change of seating partners. I noticed the plug in his ear and wondered if he was deaf, then saw the wire connected to the cassette radio which bulged his jacket pocket.

I wished that I had brought something to read. I'd left the house in such a hurry that I had taken only my shopping purse, a thin bag on a long strap that held just my keys and wallet. I pushed the button that was supposed to make the chair recline. Nothing happened. I jabbed it again and this time the back did move, too quickly. Behind me, someone spluttered a curse. "Sorry," I muttered. Gentler this time, I raised the seat a bit and lay my head back against the slippery plastic headrest.

The whistle of tires on sanded pavement and the steady hum and rock of the bus lulled me. I didn't sleep, but lay there with my eyes closed, stiffly conscious of each accidental brush of the man's thigh against my own and the pressure of his shoulder and arm as he turned the pages. After more than an hour's steady drive, the bus stopped at a suburban shopping mall and the two women got out, twittering excitedly now over the possibilities of sales and bargains. I slipped across into the vacated window seat and this time did fall into an uneasy doze, aware of our halting progress along the expressway clogged with the usual morning traffic tie-ups. Not for the first time, I wondered how people who made this drive twice a day, day after day after day, managed to remain sane.

At last, the bus pulled into the terminal. It emptied quickly. The towers of the Eaton Centre and the Bay Street financial district loomed over the shabby gray stone building, its waiting room crowded with passengers and derelicts looking for a place to get warm. Only one of the phone booths had an intact directory. I debated phoning for an appointment first but decided on surprise. The office I was looking for was on a small street off Queen East near Sherbourne. I decided to walk down Bay to Queen where I could catch the streetcar. As I dodged pedestrians and deliverymen carrying sacks of groceries to the Chinese restaurants that lined Elizabeth Street, I practised what I would say to the receptionist, the secretary, and Whitman himself.

The streetcar was crowded with a mixture of school children and workers headed to a myriad of jobs. I stood, wedged in the centre aisle and clutching the overhead bar to keep my balance against the fitful stops and starts. The windows, shut against the cold, steamed with all our breaths.

I missed Sherbourne and had to walk back two blocks, my head bent against the wind. At the corner, I stepped over two people, sexless in long gray overcoats and woollen caps pulled down to their noses, who slept bundled together like stray kittens over a sidewalk vent. Across the street, a woman pushed a baby carriage into the park. It was piled high with old newspapers, a bulging green sac wedged between its axles. I could hear her singing above the shrill keening of the wind. Someone else rooted desultorily through a wire garbage pail; others sat hunched on benches or lay like these two in the dirt, comatose, heedless of the thin snow that was beginning to fall.

The building that housed the firm of Rumble and Whitman was one of a series of Edwardian red brick warehouses that an enterprising architect had transformed into prestigious professional offices. The lawyers were on the fifth floor. The elevator was a slightly modernized version of a freight lift. The door slid down with a bang and when I pulled the lever the whole thing shook and groaned before creaking upwards. I thought of all the stories I had ever heard: of being trapped in the small dark room, of the sudden jolt before the plummet and the crash. I wondered if it was true that, if you jumped up as the elevator fell, you could save yourself.

The fifth floor appeared to be deserted. I walked down the long hallway, my boot heels clopping on varnished pine boards. Staggered on either side were doors of frosted glass, some with discrete nameplates, most bare. The office I was looking for was towards the end of the hall near the stairs. The survivor had not yet removed his partner's name from the sign. The glass glowed with light and I could hear the chatter of a computer printer. I knocked and waited.

No one answered. I knocked again, louder this time, and called out. The machine stopped. I banged on the glass and then looked back down the hall. There was no sign of activity, no one opening any door to see what the commotion was all about. I tried the handle and, to my surprise, the door swung open.

A woman sat with her back to me at a long low desk, earphones clamped over a head of wildly teased, unnaturally black hair. Lights winked on a telephone console beside her. She ignored them too. She was typing rapidly on a computer keyboard, its monitor screen shrouded by an opaque plastic cover. Her eyes were closed.

The office was the usual mix of comfort and efficiency. Directly in front of the door was the working centre: the reception desk and a bank of files in an L-shaped arrangement. To one side was a black leather sofa grouped with a pair of matching armchairs around a marble-topped coffee table laden with an untidy assortment of travel and business magazines. Framed by vivid green foliage, an immense fish tank bubbled away against the opposite wall. Beside it, another door, which probably led to the inner offices, was closed, its pebbled glass window dark. There were no pictures, and the striped vertical blinds shut out the view.

I stood by the desk and cleared my throat loudly. The typist still didn't hear me. Finally, I reached over and tentatively tapped her shoulder.

She jumped, yanking the earphones away by the thin wire that led to a desk drawer. "You scared me," she gasped. "Who are you?"

She smoothed a hand over her hair, down across the padded shoulders of a black blouse cut low to suggest a cleavage although she was far too thin for any such abundance of flesh. She was young, apparently not long out of high school. Under the heavily painted eyebrows, her black eyes peered through a thicket of mascaraed lashes. Even her lipstick was black. A triangular silver earring weighed down the lobe of one ear while the other was studded with a semicircle of seven black stones.

"I'm sorry. I didn't mean to frighten you."

"What do you want?"

"I'm here to see Mr. Whitman."

"Do you have an appointment?" She flipped through the pages of the large desk calendar, looking for the date.

"No. I happened to be in town and thought I'd drop by to pay my condolences."

"He's a very busy man." She shut the book. "You can't see him without an appointment. I'll pass along your message. And who did you say you are?" She picked up a gold pen.

"I'll only take a minute of his time," I pleaded.

She licked her lips, tasting the black liner that emphasized their fullness. "He's not here right now. Whom may I say has called?"

"Perhaps you can tell me when he'll be in?"

"He's away," she answered shortly. "There's been a death in the firm."

"I know. That's what I've come to see him about."

"Are you from the police?"

"No, nothing like that. I'm a friend of a friend."

"Oh?"

"Simon Harper. Perhaps you knew him or his wife? They were good friends of Ms. Rumble."

"It's awful, what's happened," she said. She put down the pen. "But I'm afraid I can't help you. Mr. Whitman had to go out of town on business. He won't be back for another week." She gestured at the machines. "I'm just finishing up some dictation that can't wait, then I'm off on holiday myself. He's given me the time off with pay. You're lucky you found anyone here at all."

"Could you tell me where he's gone?"

"I'm not supposed to." She opened the appointment calendar again, closed it, patted its top. "Well, since you're Mr. Harper's friend, I guess I can tell you. Mr. Whitman went down to his place in Florida right after Ms. Rumble died. He's still there."

"After she died?"

"Maybe it was just before. He missed her funeral, I know that."

"And he hasn't been back?"

"No. Did you meet him at the Harper's house?"

"I'm not sure. I'm not very good with names and faces," I smiled, but she didn't respond. "He's a short, dark-haired man, right?"

She shook her head. "He is short but he's got curly red hair.

And one of those beards." She cupped her chin, her fingers stroking to a point. "A goat, or something?"

"Goatee?"

"That's right. And long sideburns too. I keep telling him to get rid of those, they're so sixties, but he's kind of set in his ways." She flipped open a notepad. "Leave your name and I'll make sure he knows you called."

"Rosalie Cairns," I told her.

She glanced up at me through the thicket of her hair before writing the name down. I watched her underline it before she slammed the book shut.

"You're the one who found Ms. Rumble's body, aren't you?" she asked.

I nodded.

"She was so nice, not like Miss La-de-dah Simpson."

"I didn't realize Diane went by her maiden name."

"Oh yes, quite the libber that one, until it came to office work. Then it was 'Cheryl, do this,' and 'Cheryl, do that,' and always right away, no excuses. She never had one single thing to say to me, personal-like you know."

"She worked here? In this office?"

"She and her husband had their own business, travel I think. He ran it, but she was the one with the money. She was in here all the time, talking to Mr. Whitman and Ms. Rumble. I didn't know any of them very well. I only got the job six months ago when the other secretary left, for Florida actually. Mr. Whitman is setting up a branch office down there for all the snowbirds. Now that's a job offer I wouldn't turn down. Are you a lawyer, too?"

"No," I said. "Thanks for your help. I'm sorry to have bothered you."

"No problem. I'll tell Mr. Whitman you came by when he calls." She looked at her watch. "He usually checks in about lunchtime."

"Don't bother," I said. "I'll probably see him at the

Harper's funeral. It was nothing important."

She shrugged. "It's your business." She turned back to the keyboard and her fingers began their tap dance once again.

This time, there were plenty of seats on the streetcar. I went into the Eaton Centre to get warm and to decide what to do next. It was hard to deal with the disappointment of discovering that Whitman had been out of the country when the Harpers died. I had convinced myself that he was the culprit and that confronting him would end the series of accidents that had arisen since I found Jennifer Rumble's body. I didn't want to admit, even to myself, that Finlay may have been right and that this trip was a waste of time.

It was not just the deaths of strangers that depressed me. I contemplated dropping into the library, but couldn't face my old friends' questions, their curiosity about this sudden visit and about small town life in general. When I left my job there, all my co-workers had been enthusiastic in their insistence that I return to see them. The few times I had visited, I found little to talk about with them, preoccupied as they were with their business and the turf wars of office politics. I didn't belong there any more.

My back ached and, as I trudged through the mall, sharp pains pulled at the backs of my legs. I wanted to go home, to sleep for a week.

There was a noon bus, a milk run that stopped at every commuter housing development and small town on Highway 7 on the way back home. I took it anyway, reasoning that it wouldn't be full. Within minutes of leaving the city, I was asleep to wake only vaguely at each stop until the bus pulled into the terminal. "All out," the driver shouted. I stumbled down the steps, welcoming his hand at my elbow.

The afternoon was raw and gray, cars splashing sheets of slush up on the sidewalks. There were no cabs in sight. I thought about phoning Will, but finally decided to walk home, hoping the fresh air would wake me up. I didn't go through the park but crossed the river on one of the two concrete bridges that connected the downtown to my neighbourhood streets. I simply walked, head bent, thinking only of a hot bath and clean sheets.

Sadie wasn't in the yard or in the house though her leash hung from its customary hook by the back door. I called Will's shop in a panic. For once he was in, and picked up the phone himself.

"What are you doing home already?" he demanded. "Why didn't you call? I would have come and picked you up at the station."

"Never mind about me. Sadie's disappeared." I began to cry.

"Calm down. She's all right. I took her back to the vet's this morning. They need to run some more tests, so are going to keep her overnight. She's had a bad reaction to those sedatives. Dr. DuMaurier has put her on something different. She'll be fine in a day or two."

"I was so worried to find the house empty. I thought Matty might have come back and really hurt her this time."

"We don't know it was him for sure," Will cautioned.

"I know." I wiped my eyes with my sleeve. "I'm not feeling well, I think I've got flu or something. I'm going to bed."

"What happened in Toronto?"

"Nothing."

"You didn't find Whitman?"

"He's in Florida. Turns out he has been there for quite some time."

"That takes care of that then." Will sighed. "I'm going to be late tonight. I thought you were going to stay overnight in the city, so I made some plans."

"It doesn't matter. I'm just going to sleep."

He hung up. I gently cradled the phone. He hadn't told me his plans for that evening. I shook myself angrily. He always had customers who preferred to meet after dinner. Late business hours were nothing out of the ordinary. I had to stop feeling sorry for myself, stop imagining things about Will. I was just disappointed that I hadn't solved the big mystery with one coup. That is, if there was a mystery to solve.

I hauled myself up the stairs and turned on the hot water in the bath.

FOURTEEN

I woke up in the pitch dark. Someone stumbled against the door and cursed. I switched on the bedside lamp. Will stood there, rubbing his knee.

"Sorry," he mumbled, "I tried not to wake you."

"You've been drinking."

He straightened up, tried to pull off his sweatshirt, lost his balance and staggered back against the wall. "Me and the boys quaffed a few," he said. "Well, me and Jerry did."

He dropped his clothes on the floor where he stood. He almost fell getting into bed. I made room for him. He was breathing so heavily, I thought he'd passed out. After a moment, however, he managed to get himself under the duvet. He curled into my warmth, his feet icy on my calves.

"What was the occasion?" I asked.

"Marbella," he said. "He wants me to plan and supervise all the kitchens and bathrooms for those six new houses he's putting up by the golf course. He wants the craftsman's touch."

"So, now I can congratulate you."

"It's going to mean a lot of work. It's not like doing a job on my own with Jerry's help. There's six houses with six kitchens and at least twelve bathrooms. That means I'll need a crew. That means a lot more paperwork, supervision rather than construction. I'll have Marbella breathing down my neck about costs. I won't be able to set my own hours and everything will have to be okayed each step of the way."

"You don't have to do it."

"I know. But there's the challenge. And the money. And if everything works out as it should and they all get done on time, Marbella hinted at more contracts, bigger ones. This could be it for me, Rosie."

I stroked his arm. "You're freezing. I'll get the hot water bottle."

Stepping on the cold tiles of the bathroom floor was like treading on ice. I let the water run almost to boiling, filled the bottle, and turned out the light as I came back into the room.

When I got back into bed, Will hugged me close. "I love you," he whispered.

"Isn't that sweet," a voice said from the doorway.

In silhouette against the dim square of the hall window loomed the black shadow of a man.

"Who are you?" Will shouted. "How did you get in?"

"With the key, of course. It's a nice place," he leaned casually against the doorjamb. In one hand, he held a small gun, aimed straight at us. "I liked it a lot. Too bad my little friend got carried away, but I can see you've tidied up. I like to see someone take pride in their home. That," he gestured with the weapon towards the remnants of wallpaper, "that was really unnecessary, and I do apologize."

"What do you want?" I whispered.

He bowed. "You ask me that? Dear Rosalie." He switched the overhead light back on. I blinked against the glare. It was the man I'd met in the park.

"But who are you?" I almost screamed my frustration.

"John Whitman," he bowed, his left hand sweeping off an imaginary hat while the other kept the gun aimed quite steadily.

"Your secretary said you had red hair and a beard."

"The wonders of modern technology. Haven't you ever heard of a razor and dye? You think I'd be stupid enough to come here without some kind of disguise?"

"What are you doing here?"

"I've come for Jennifer's diary, of course. Where is it?"

"The police have it," Will said.

"They have the file from Dunstable's car?" When we both nodded, he continued, "That's not what I want. I want her red leather address book, her journal. You know what I mean."

"All we've ever seen is the file in Finlay's office," Will repeated.

Whitman sighed and brandished the gun. "Must we keep playing games?" he demanded. "Why don't you just give it to me and let me get on with it."

"We've got nothing to give you." In spite of the danger, I was beginning to get angry.

Will added, "I hadn't seen her in years and she was dead when Rosie found her. She gave us nothing."

"She knew you lived here," Whitman chided. "We passed your shop a couple of times on our little trips. She liked to keep tabs on people, you know. Are you trying to tell me she never contacted you?"

"She never called us," Will asserted.

"You're lying." Whitman spat the words. "I found your phone number in her file the day before she came up here. That's when I learned she kept a journal record of the names and addresses of everyone we dealt with: those who got the babies, those who didn't, those who took care of sales. I told her to get rid of it, that it was too dangerous. She wouldn't listen to me. She said she would get help from a real friend — you."

Will continued to shake his head. He clutched my hand for strength and for support. "She never called," he repeated.

Whitman turned to me. "Then you met her. She phoned here and you arranged to meet her by the river. She gave the book to you."

I couldn't speak. In his fist, the gun remained steady, its black mouth open and waiting. I inched myself closer to Will, my arms still clutching the hot water bottle in the folds of my long cotton gown.

"What's in the file, anyway? Finlay says it's in code." Will tried to keep the conversation commonplace as if that could ward off danger.

"Business records." Whitman answered. "I may as well tell you the whole story. You work for yourself, you understand my pleasure in a good deal and how upset I am that it's been ruined."

Will put his arm around me. I wondered if Whitman was talking to us because he knew we wouldn't be able to tell on him. The grave holds all secrets.

He leaned casually against the wall. The gun did not waver. "We had such a good business going, the four of us," he said. "I handled the distribution; Simon and Diane had the contacts down south; Jennifer found the marks up here. She had access to clinic records through some doctor. She was good at identifying who was likely to go for our deal, and got them to pay substantial fees for hospital, infant care, a little something for the "mothers," bribes, things like that. Then we'd bring them in."

"The babies?"

"Some babies. We couldn't always get enough of them."

"But what about the picture . . ." I stopped too late.

Whitman grinned. "Met the Lorings, did you? Or Mrs. Dunstable showed it to you? What a pathetic woman. That baby was adopted two years ago. A couple in Saskatoon have her, a very rich, very lovely couple. It's a useful photo though, don't you think? Such an appealing brat."

"How can you use the same baby picture over and over again? What about the people who think they're getting her? The Lorings are threatening to go to the police and Mrs. Dunstable knows your connection with the whole affair."

"They have nothing on paper, nothing signed with our names. We say the mother's changed her mind, but that the money's gone on bribes. Or that the kid's dead. It doesn't really matter. Most of the people who come to us are desperate and used to disappointment. Besides, the Harpers did provide babies often enough to keep real trouble away. We did have a success rate. Of sorts."

"Didn't you care about the pain you were causing?"

He shrugged. "It made a good cover, the baby business. The real money is in drugs. We used little baby mules," he barked a laugh. "Guys I defended agreed to work for me. That's how we came here in the first place. The Dunstable boy was a natural, wouldn't you say? His old man really pissed me off, with his holier-than-thou attitude. I can't stand attitudes. Then, when his wife appeared at the clinic, it was a Godsend. So to speak." He snickered.

"Did you know they stole the money to pay for the baby?" I asked.

He shrugged. "They were too poor for us to consider for our service otherwise. It was the old lady's idea. Jennifer went along with it for awhile. She got cold feet, too late as usual."

"Why?"

"The silly bitch developed a conscience. She wanted to save the boy, or some such nonsense. She came to see you," he said suddenly, pointing the gun at Will.

Will shook his head. "We've told you everything we know. What do you want from us now?"

"You're getting in my way." His voice turned colder. He wasn't joking any more. "Cheryl told me that Rosalie was nosing around the office. I'm almost ready to get out of here for good, but I need some more time. You are going to be my little diversion. Now get out of bed. One at a time."

"Why?" Will asked, not moving.

"I need that journal and you're going to give it to me."

"We don't have it." Will almost screamed in rage.

Whitman shrugged again. "Too bad. I'll have to look elsewhere for it. Now, let's get this business over with. Out."

Will stood up first. "Let me get dressed," he muttered. Whitman grinned, but nodded. Will picked up his pants. The other man whistled. Will flushed but what he muttered was inaudible. He took a long time to find a shirt. Whitman watched him, one foot lightly tapping the floor.

Quickly I put my arms behind my back, unscrewing the bottle stopper and holding it carefully upright. The steam pasted the fabric to my spine. I crawled out of the duvet, allowing my gown to slip over one shoulder.

"What's the point in hurting us? We won't tell anyone you were here. You can just go and forget about us." My voice rose in a whine.

Whitman laughed. "Oh, sure. I have as much trust for you as I had for my precious partners. And don't think your tits will turn me on. Diane found that that doesn't work with me."

"You killed her." Will said softly.

"She was doing too much dope. Getting careless. I don't like loose ends, things should be left neat and tidy." He smirked. "I made certain that Diane told her aunt that she thought you were involved with Jennifer and I made sure to pass on an 'anonymous' tip that your car was in the church parking lot where Dunstable was found. The cops are already wondering about you two. Murder-suicide is rather neat, don't you think? A nice touch of guilt and remorse. A perfect red herring to buy me another couple of weeks to find what I came here for. I'd burn this house, but my little helper has taken off and I like things to look natural. Arson's not my specialty, accidents are."

He cocked the gun. Will dived for the floor. I whipped the bottle towards the door. The scalding water hit Whitman full in the face. He screamed and dropped the gun, but not before his finger hit the trigger.

An explosion of light and sound rocked the room. Plaster rained from the ceiling. Will leaped, and the two men crashed to the floor. I was off the bed and grabbing for the gun, trying to avoid their flailing arms and legs. We were all yelling.

Whitman broke away and ran for the stairs. Will caught his ankle and he toppled, shrieking once as he bounced down. Then there was only Will, his arms around me, the room loud with our sobs.

"I'll call the cops," Will finally said. He nudged aside a large square of plaster that was soaking up the water. "I guess it's time to replace the ceiling too."

In spite of everything, I grinned, then bit my lips before laughter could turn to hysteria.

Will hugged me again. "You'd better keep an eye on our visitor."

Whitman lay at the foot of the stairs, one leg bent at an acute angle from the knee, the bone sticking white through his pant leg, the rug turning red beneath him. He cursed in a low steady hiss, his eyes screwed tight shut against the hall light.

I crouched on the landing, clutching the gun in both hands. I was afraid to touch any of the levers in case it went off again. I couldn't deal with any more destruction.

"Rosalie," Whitman's whisper was urgent and sudden.

I almost dropped the gun. I looked towards the study where Will could be heard demanding to speak to Finlay.

"I didn't do it," he said.

"Do what?"

"Kill Dunstable. Or Jennifer, for that matter."

"You expect me to believe you? And what about the Harpers?"

"They deserved to die." He grimaced. "They were both screwing up, making a mess of things." He caught his breath. "But not Jennifer, I wouldn't hurt her. Someone else did her and Dunstable. I got to the church too late. I did see another car drive off."

Probably us, I thought. I looked down at him, considering.

"Save it for the cops," Will interjected. He leaned over the railing and smiled in triumph at the wreck below.

"You've got to listen to me, Rosalie," Whitman insisted. He deliberately ignored Will. "Ask Will where he was when Jennifer died. Ask him what happened to her address book, whose name is in there. Go on, ask him." He tried to raise himself on one elbow but fell back with a groan. Sirens whooped in the distance.

"She knows the truth," Will declared. "She knows I've got nothing left to hide."

I looked up at him, his face red from the strain of the fight, his knuckles white on the bannister.

"You've already told us that Diane planted rumours with Miss Simpson," I said to Whitman. "You expect me to believe your lies about him now?"

"I didn't do it," Whitman said again. "I would never have killed her here, so close to the Dunstables and my distribution network. I wouldn't put my whole scheme into such danger on purpose."

"Don't listen to him, Rosie," Will commanded.

The sirens screamed to a stop outside our house. Feet pounded on the porch and fists battered the door. Will ran downstairs past me, stepped over Whitman's prone body, and opened the door. Police invaded the hall. One pulled Will into the living room while another knelt by the wounded man. Finlay came up the stairs and took the gun from me. I put my face in my hands. He went into the bedroom and came back with the duvet. He draped it over my shoulders before going back downstairs to deal with the ambulance and to direct McPhail in her search for evidence. When she passed me on her way to our room, she let one hand rest for a moment on my shoulder. I was glad that she didn't speak. I couldn't have talked to anyone just then.

A little later, when the excitement calmed and most of the police left, Finlay sat with us in the living room. Someone had made a pot of tea. I gulped the welcome warmth.

"So this is where Whitman ended up," Finlay said.

"You've been looking for him?" Will asked.

"We're not stupid," Finlay replied. "Once we made the connection between the Harpers and Rumble, it was obvious that Whitman must be involved somehow. He was her law partner after all. I had one talk with him back when Rumble was found. He seemed shook up, but not surprised. I had the city cops keep an eye on him until he dropped out of sight. His secretary said he was down in Florida."

"That's what she told Rosie too," Will interrupted

Finlay cocked his head at me. "You went down to Whitman's office in the city? I thought I told you to stay out of trouble."

"It didn't matter," I mumbled. "He was here all along."

"So it appears." Finlay covered a yawn. "We found out one of his old clients was living here and we have reason to suspect he was dealing drugs. You know that fellow lives in the same building as your friend? Gary Donnelly."

"Gary took off with Matty Dunstable," Will announced.

"I know. We've got a warrant out for them. Suspicion. Someone saw a truck looks an awful lot like that new Chevy Donnelly drives in the chapel parking lot the night before we found Dunstable's body."

"You think Matty might have killed his own father?" I put the cup down on the table before it spilled and gripped my hands together to still their shaking.

Finlay shrugged. "Possibly. The two of them didn't get on very well. We haven't closed the book on Dunstable's death yet. Finding the file with him is a puzzle. Who put it there? If he did himself, where's the missing journal? Besides the business with the exhaust pipe, there was enough valium in his bloodstream to knock him out. Same as Rumble. Then we have what happened to the Harpers. Suicide and accident."

"Whitman said he arranged accidents," Will put in.

Finlay nodded. "We're sure we can link him to the

Harpers' deaths. A car like the one parked out front was noticed that night. It's rented in the name of Joe White, a pretty obvious pseudonym. And then there's the boy. He's got quite a record already: disturbing the peace, vandalism, you name it. We suspect he's been behind a couple of suspicious fires over the last year or two."

"He was the one who trashed our house," I said. "Whitman pretty well admitted it."

"Doesn't surprise me." Finlay smothered another yawn. "We think he's involved with the local drug trade. He and Donelly made regular trips to Toronto, and always spent some time in a bar on Sherbourne near Whitman's office. The old man was strict; maybe he threatened the boy, or Rumble did, so the kid took care of them both. Maybe Dunstable killed Rumble because he thought she had a hand in corrupting his son, then killed himself out of remorse."

"Maybe there's a third murderer you haven't thought of yet," I said.

Will Whitman sighed. "That kind of thinking will get you into more trouble. Is that what you want?"

"No."

"I'll go talk to Whitman. He's got no choice except to confess after what went down here tonight. Where's your dog by the way?"

"I had to take her back to the vet's for more tests," Will explained.

"Really? Poor thing. I hope she's okay. If she'd been here, she might have scared him off. Or at least given you some warning."

"If she'd been here, he probably would have killed her this time," I said.

"Maybe. You were pretty lucky. A hot water bottle," he snorted. "Never would have guessed it."

"What happens now?" Will asked.

Finlay shrugged. "Once Whitman pleads guilty, it's all over. I can't believe that he'll go to trial, given his attack on you and evidence at the Harper scene. He'll be in prison for quite a while in any case, that I can assure you."

He stood up, stretching and not bothering to hide another yawn. "You take care of yourself now," he said to me. "I don't want to see you again, unless it's to fix a parking ticket." He laughed at the expressions on our faces. "Only joking. I'm exhausted. The baby's got colic and the next youngest is teething. I can't remember when I last had a full night's sleep."

Will saw him out the door, then went into the kitchen. I struggled out of the nest of blankets I'd made on the couch and joined him there.

"Do you think it's all over?" I asked him.

"I hope so." He rummaged in the cupboard for the bottle of scotch we kept for special occasions. "I need a drink." He poured two generous measures and handed one to me. "To the end of all our troubles."

He clicked my glass with his with too much force. The liquor slopped over the edge and down my sleeve. The acrid scent of whiskey filled the room.

"Oh well," I licked my wrist.

Will caught my hand and kissed it. "It's finished," he said. "We can go back to our normal lives. Finlay is convinced of Whitman's guilt."

"And you believe him?"

He shrugged. "He's the expert."

"True." I stared at him, watching my image fill and waver in his eyes. I cupped his head in my hands and drew his face down to my mouth. We kissed for a long, long time. Then, hand in hand, we went upstairs to bed.

FIFTEEN

The phone rang early the next morning. "I just heard the news," Karen cried. "They caught the guy."

"Which guy?" I wasn't fully awake. I could hear the sound of the shower and Will's tremendous sighs as he scrubbed.

"Whitman. The one who's been doing all the killing," she said. "They've charged him with arson and murder in the Harper case and suspicion in the Rumble death. They say it's not suicide after all."

"What about Dunstable?"

"Dunstable?" She was clearly puzzled. "But that was suicide. Anyway they didn't say anything about him."

"Has Cindy heard from Gary at all?"

"No. And she's not expecting to now. There's a warrant out for him and Matty."

"I know. How's she doing?"

"Not too well. She doesn't know what to do about the baby and she's just lost her job. Apparently Gary was skimming money from the station and his uncle won't believe she had nothing to do with it, so he fired her."

"She needs a good lawyer."

"Contradiction in terms," Karen laughed. "Seriously though, the poor kid is in bad shape. Her father won't have anything to do with her at all and her mother blames her for getting involved with a man like Gary in the first place. She says that Cindy should at least have had the sense to get married. As if that would have changed anything."

"I just had an idea." I said. "Would she give the baby up for adoption?"

"She wants to, but she's heard so many horror stories about foster care. She wants to be able to visit the baby and watch her grow up. Not interfere, but be there for it, if it wants her."

"Let me talk to Will, and then get back to you."

"Rosie, that would be perfect, you taking her baby."

"Not me," I was indignant. "I'll call you later."

Will was drying his hair when I burst into the bathroom.

"I've just had a great idea," I said.

"Why does that worry me?" he grinned.

"No, listen. That was Karen on the phone, talking about Cindy and all the trouble she's in now. Especially with this baby coming along. What do you think about introducing her to the Lorings? They'd be perfect parents for the baby, and I know they'd welcome Cindy into their family too. Some good would come out of all this."

"Not a bad idea at all," Will agreed. He rubbed his head with the towel. "What about us?"

"Taking the baby?" I sat down on the edge of the tub.

"It's an idea," he said. He stared into the mirror.

"I'm not ready. It's too soon. Besides, the Lorings already have the nursery decorated."

"All right." He turned and hugged me. "Who needs to stay up all night anyway? Finlay is an object lesson for all us want-to-be parents."

I realized suddenly that Will's head seemed to be swelling and shrinking as the bathroom light dimmed and brightened. I put my hand out to clutch the sink.

"What's wrong?" Will asked.

"I think I'm going to be sick," I said. And I was.

He helped me to my feet. "Oh my God," he said.

"What's wrong?"

"You're covered in blood."

I started to cry.

"Where does it hurt?" He began to pat me all over with light anxious touches. "A bullet must have nicked you. Couldn't you feel anything? Do you think we should go to the hospital?"

I pushed him away. "We don't have to go anywhere," I said. "It's just my period. Again."

"Shock," announced Karen. She stirred a teabag around with a wooden stick in a styrofoam cup. I sipped my coffee. It tasted sour and oily. Flecks of cream clotted along the rim. I put it down on the floor.

We were working together today. The Christmas rush had started and Dr. Long insisted that we double our shifts to try to cut down on shoplifting and to keep the shelves fully stocked. New books were arriving daily, as the publishers exploited their most profitable season with instant bestsellers and unreadable, but handsomely produced, coffee table books. One of us worked unpacking and shelving while the other dealt with the endless stream of questioning, querulous customers.

I felt sick, and had trouble keeping myself from snapping at one woman who could not choose between two cheap paperbacks for her daughter's stocking. "Take both," I finally suggested. She left with neither.

Karen nipped across the street, dodging the traffic and skipping over the snowdrifts banked in the gutters. When she came back with two steaming cups, I put the "Back in 5 Minutes" sign on the door. We retired to the basement where we perched on trestles left over from the building renovation.

"So," Karen shook her head. "You caught the bad guy and now it's all over."

"I hope so." I swirled the brown stuff in my cup. Upstairs, someone banged on the door. We listened for a moment, but whoever it was went away. "I wish I could have stayed home today. I'm feeling lousy, and of course I didn't get much sleep. I couldn't reach Lil, and Stephanie refused to come in. She's working on her job resume."

"Why don't you go home? I can handle the store by myself, I've done it often enough. You're the boss now, you can take time off when you need it."

I shook my head. "It's probably better to be busy doing something then sitting around moping. As you say, it's all over. So Finlay assures us. Will seems to believe him."

"You don't?"

"Well, I can't understand why Whitman would insist he had nothing to do with Jennifer Rumble's death when he was willing to admit to killing the Harpers. And why he was still looking for her diary. The police don't have it. We've never seen it. There's also the Reverend. Somehow I still can't believe he killed himself."

"Didn't Finlay say they thought Matty might have done that?"

"That's what he said. But you saw Matty that day and you said he seemed normal, cheerful even. The kid was a little creep, true, but I find it hard to believe that even he could be joking around so soon after killing his own father. No, I think Matty and Gary were behind the drug dealing, no question there, but I don't think they had anything to do with the Reverend's death."

"Gary's truck was there."

"A witness said it looked like Gary's truck. Lots of people drive trucks."

"But lots of people don't have motives to kill. Besides, didn't Dunstable have one of Rumble's files with him? Maybe he killed her, then killed himself because he couldn't stand the guilt."

"That's what Will thinks." I wandered into the bathroom and poured the coffee down the drain. It swirled in bubbles around the stained porcelain sink before disappearing with a distinct glug. I swallowed bile. I will not throw up, I told myself fiercely.

"You don't agree?"

"I don't know. It seems so out of character. When he came to see us that day, the Reverend was really upset about Rumble and her missing file. If he had it already, why would he ask us about it? He was very worried, but not for himself."

"Maybe he realized Matty was in deep trouble."

"There's something else," I said. "Something I didn't tell you before. When I talked to Mrs. Dunstable, she implied that Dr. Long was involved as well."

"Our Dr. Long?"

I nodded. "Mrs. Dunstable went to a fertility clinic in Toronto. She wouldn't tell me which one, or who she saw, but when I suggested Dr. Long's name, she didn't say no. And later, when he was telling us about the scheme, Whitman said that Jennifer found the names of marks through a doctor."

I don't know why I didn't tell her about Will's confession to me about his talks with Dr. Long and Jennifer Rumble. I hadn't decided yet which hurt worse: his going behind my back to discuss adoption when he knew my feelings about it, or his decision to keep that discussion secret after I found the lawyer's body.

"What does Finlay say?"

I shrugged. "Just that he's looking into it. It could be an innocent connection. If Dr. Long is found guilty, though, I wonder what will happen to this store and our jobs?"

More pounding on the door. Karen drained her tea. "Well, whatever's going to happen, will happen. For now, we'd better get back to work."

I unlocked the door for the impatient customer, a man looking for war memoirs. More customers arrived. Karen took a turn at the till while I shelved books in the back corner, taking the chance to rest by sitting on the floor. Few people bothered

browsing this far back. One woman did stop. I looked up to see
Miss Simpson hovering over me.

"I just came to say good-bye." Her smile didn't reach her
eyes. For the first time since I'd met her, she wore no make-up
and a plain black coat opened to reveal a gray wool suit.

I scrambled to my feet. "I'm so sorry about Diane. And
Simon." I lifted my hand to touch her, but let it fall.

"Thank you. Diane was very dear to me and I, for one, will
miss her greatly." She blinked rapidly and looked away.

"Are you going away?" I wanted to change the subject.

"Moving," she sighed. "The big house is too much for me.
Geoffrey has found me a very lovely apartment in the city in one
of those retirement condominiums. It's a new building on a quiet
street, a short walk away from shopping and church and the
subway. It's not far from both my brothers' homes so I'll have
company." She gazed around the store. "I always liked coming
in here. You girls were always so friendly. In the big city, you
never know what store clerks might be like."

"I'm sure you'll be happy there," I said.

She sniffed and brushed at her eyes. "Not happy," she said.
"Not now. But comfortable. I've sold the cottage land too.
Maybe I'll go to Florida with Geoffrey and Linda this year. I
don't know." Her lips trembled.

Karen called me. "Can you take over, Rosie? I've got to go
downstairs for a minute."

I smiled apologetically at Miss Simpson. She waved her
hand in vague understanding. "Good-bye," I said to her.

She nodded. A few minutes later, she left the store without
buying anything.

"What was that all about?" Karen asked in the next pause
between customers.

I told her.

"I can't say I'm sorry to see her leave," she said. "But the
way she's carrying on, you'd think she was Diane's mother."

"Excuse me for interrupting your talk," said one of two women who had just bustled into the store.

"I want a book," the other spoke angrily, as if we were accusing her of some sin. "I don't know the title, but the author was on TV the other day. It has a blue cover." She looked at us expectantly.

"Animal, mineral or vegetable?" Karen asked and we both began to laugh. The women stomped out, offended.

Christmas brought its usual rush of sales followed in January by three dreary days of counting stock. Then business settled down to its usual winter lull. Although there was no concrete evidence linking her to the scheme, I wasn't surprised when Dr. Long moved, apparently permanently, to Curaçao. Her nephew, Ernest Long, was now taking care of the accounts. I knew I would have to make up my mind about staying on as manager. As long as things remained relatively the same — Stephanie and Lil and Karen and I working shifts, Ernest collecting the monthly receipts — I drifted.

Cindy and the Lorings agreed on the adoption; in fact, they began attending birth classes together. She got a temporary job frying burgers in a fast food restaurant. She was determined to pay Gary's debts before going back to school in the fall.

John Whitman pleaded guilty to arson and murder in the Harper case, drug dealing, and attacking us. He refused to admit to any responsibility for what happened to Rumble and Dunstable; their deaths are officially suicides. He wrote me a letter, but I returned it unanswered. Gary Donnelly and Matty Dunstable stayed missing.

I strolled home from work, my jacket open and my face turned to the breeze which smelled of bared earth, spring coming. At six o'clock the sun was just beginning to set, the sky still a clear cold blue, gathering gray at its edges. An early thaw had melted most of the snow; water dripped from tree branches and swirled in the gutters, while salt and sand still gritted underfoot on the sidewalk. Lawns were dotted with pools of mud churned up by children racing after balls and driving their bikes pell-mell through the neighbourhood. Two policemen sitting on the steps of the station nodded to me as I passed by.

I leaned over the bridge railing, watching the lazy swirl of the river. Only one sluice of the dam was open, the fall a muffled grumble. Ducks, roosting on the log boom that kept trash away from the hydro outlets, ruffled their feathers. Two drakes, seeing me there, swam over to investigate the possibilities of bread crusts. Two more quacked in for a landing. As I crossed the park towards home, blackbirds trilled in the alders along the river bank; swallows soared and spun. A killdeer shot up from the long grass by the abandoned railway line and skimmed away from its nest with its luring cry. At the top of the hill, I turned to watch the sun set, a great red wash splashed across the sky, the steeple of St. John's pointing one long finger at the white clouds massing above.

Stuffed in the mailbox were three thick envelopes addressed to me, applications for doctoral programs in English Literature. I put them on the kitchen counter unopened while I checked the recipes I planned to use for a four-course curry meal, a spring celebration. As I chopped and assembled spices, onions, garlic and ginger, I stopped to thumb through the pages of the accompanying calendars with their photographs of small intent classes and beautiful buildings of ivy covered stone. I reread course descriptions and thesis requirements.

I ate dinner alone, putting Will's under foil in the oven. He didn't bother calling any more when he was going to be late, such a regular occurrence I wondered why I kept cooking meals for him at all. I left the applications on the table and went up to run a bath. I had the new P.D. James and was reading murder in the tub when he got home.

"Hi," he shouted up the stairs. "It's me."

I turned on more hot water. I heard him get his plate from the oven, the scrape of the chair as he sat down. After awhile, he came upstairs, the calendars in his hand.

"What's this?"

"Ever since you mentioned it last winter, I've been thinking about going back to school. I've decided to do it."

He turned the calendars over. "UBC? Concordia?"

I set up a wave with a flick of one foot. "I've settled on York. Toronto's not far away."

"I thought you said before that you couldn't bear the idea of commuting."

"I know. But what's the choice? I don't want to keep working for the Longs at the bookstore. Even being manager doesn't make that much difference: it's still working part time for someone else. I want a real challenge, a chance for a profession that means something to me. I'm proposing a thesis on the semiotics of murder, comparing contemporary women detective novelists in Canada, the US and Britain." I tried a laugh. "It'll justify reading all this junk." I flipped the pages of the paperback.

"You're really serious about this, aren't you?"

"Yes."

"If we had a child . . ." he began.

I sat up abruptly, a tidal wave washing over the edge of the tub. "That's not fair, and you know it. The fact is we don't have a baby, and we won't have one. We certainly aren't going to buy one! I can't wait any longer for the impossible to happen, for something to just turn up."

"You'll have to give me a minute to think about this. You've kind of sprung it on me unawares." Will rolled the calendars into a tube and tapped it against his thigh. When I reached for a towel, he backed off into the bedroom.

I found him there, sitting on the bed and turning the pages of one of the books. I sat down beside him, my hands folded in my lap.

"I've thought it all out," I said. "I'm going to cash in my RRSP and those bonds I put by when I was working in the library. I'll apply for a teaching assistantship as well. I'll try to get all my classes and teaching seminars on the same two or three days to cut down the travel. Lots of people commute from here to the city by bus."

"It's tough in winter, though," he said. "What if the highway's closed when you have to get to class? What about using the library for your research?"

"I could always stay overnight with someone if I had to."

Will put his arm around me. "Don't take this the wrong way, Rosie: have you thought of taking an apartment for yourself in the city? For during the week?"

"My own place?" Of course, I had fantasized such a solution, but couldn't believe that he was suggesting it. I had never lived alone as an adult and had always wondered what it would be like to live to no one's schedule but my own.

"You could get a small apartment near the campus," Will went on, "and on weekends you could come home here, or I could come to the city. We'd see each other less, but when we were together, we'd *be* together, no work, no worrying about business or school. It'll be like the days before we married." He ruffled my hair. "Remember those weekends? I don't think we ever went outside."

"You're not mad about this?"

"Rosie, after all these years, how can you say such a thing? You haven't been happy; we haven't been happy for a long time. If this is something you really want, then you should do it. I've got my business and though I love it, I know it's been hard on you. This way, we both get what we want and we get to stay together."

"It'll only be two years." I was excited, already thinking about what furniture I would need to take. "Once I'm finished with the course requirements, I can do the research and writing of the thesis on my own time."

"Dr. Rosalie Cairns," he drawled. "I do like the sound of that."

"I love you," I said. I hugged him.

"I love you, too. Always have, always will."

We kissed, lightly at first, a pact between companions. Our arms tightened. I was reflected in his eyes, as he in mine, the quickening pulse of our breathing the only sound in the room. The scent of soap as my robe slipped off mingled with the musky tang of his skin. Our bodies fit so well together, we made a puzzle completed.

SIXTEEN

To put an end to this entire episode, there was one more person I had to see. I had said good-bye to Miss Simpson, but I had not seen Mrs. Dunstable since that last terrible night. I was haunted by the vision of her clutching that sad photograph, rocking back and forth on the edge of the stairs. The Reverend's death remained a mystery, officially a suicide. Matty was still missing.

Even the daffodils nodding their brilliant crowns against the black earth of the garden could not relieve the grim facade of the Dunstable house. As before, I saw the quiver of the living room sheers as I walked up the path. This time my knock was answered immediately.

She stood in the doorway, arms folded across her breasts. She still wore her hair pulled back from her face in a tight knot, but the dress she wore was a gaily flowered print with fine lace collar and cuffs. It was longer than currently fashionable and was cinched around her waist with a narrow white leather belt, the hem a jaunty flare. She wore sheer stockings and white high-heeled shoes. She wasn't used to these; as she turned back into her house, she faltered, putting out her hand to grasp the newel post for support. I followed her indoors.

The house smelled of lemon oil and dust. There were a few cardboard boxes piled in the hall; the living room was empty, a pale square of hardwood marking the outline of a rug. Mrs. Dunstable walked straight through to the kitchen. It was a large room whose one window was set high up over the sink. A gray formica top table and two metal chairs upholstered in yellow plastic sat stranded in the middle of the floor. Several cupboard doors hung open, revealing bare shelves.

"I'm moving," she said suddenly, then laughed an awkward cough of amusement. "Well, that's rather obvious, isn't it? You might as well sit."

She leaned back against the counter, staring down at me. I saw now that she wore make-up, twin spots of rouge glowing on each cheek, her lips clumsily outlined in red. She saw me looking and flushed. She picked up a compact and a cotton puff from the counter behind her. "You'll excuse me while I fix my face." She rubbed at her mouth.

"I came to say I'm sorry," I began.

She clicked the compact closed. "What for?"

I gestured around me at the emptiness. "Your husband, your son."

"Nothing to do with you," she said, "I'm well out of here. I never liked this house, never. I told Ian so when he first brought me here, before Matthew was born. No good will come out of this place, I said. The windows are too small, the house faces the wrong direction. East," she threw her hand out towards the window as if that would explain her reasoning. "You need to live along the gravity lines, north to south. You can't sleep any other way, your dreams will sour. But he wouldn't listen. He never listened except to what he wanted to hear. And the boy was no better. Ah well, I'm free of it now. I've sold it all, lock, stock and barrel."

"Are you going on a trip?" I asked. On the floor were two suitcases, so new I could smell the leather.

"Why?" She asked sharply. "What's it to you?"

"I just wondered, that's all. Have you heard from Matty?"

"No."

I shifted, the taut plastic of the chair squeaking under my weight. I tried to think of something else to say, to make sense of my visit. A large white handbag yawned open on the table. I noted its contents: a small pack of tissues, a linen handkerchief which I bet myself was neatly embroidered with her initials, a gray wallet stuffed thickly with money, a plastic transparent change purse, a ring heavy with keys, a wad of newspaper coupons pinned together with a large paperclip, and a red leather journal.

Mrs. Dunstable moved her head impatiently, her breath escaping through pinched lips in an exasperated hiss. The sun now lay in a wide band across the room, its rays highlighting the gold edging of the journal's pages, the embossed initials on its spine. J.R. Jennifer Rumble.

She saw it at the same time I did. Before I could move, she had swept the bag up off the table, closing it fast over its contents and clutching it to her.

I pushed the chair back. "I'd better go."

"Sit down." Her lips were working furiously but no more words came.

I looked at the door. How was I going to get out of here?

"It's no good," she said. "I can't let you go now." She opened the bag again and pawed through its contents.

What she came up with was a brilliant blue hasp. She pushed a button and a long blade flicked out. She smiled then. "One of Matthew's toys," she purred. "I had to take it from his dresser once. His teacher had complained. His teachers were always complaining. They didn't understand him, they just made him worse. I knew, though. It was in this house. He thought he had lost his little knife. I heard him searching through his room. But he never asked me for it, never."

"My husband knows I'm here. He'll be coming for me in a few minutes."

"You're lying," she said calmly. "I can always tell when someone is lying. Like that woman, Rumble."

"*You* met her?"

"She tried to tell me my baby wasn't mine, that she belonged to someone else. She said it was all a trick, that Ian knew all about it. She said she wanted to help me. Help me! I helped her all right." Mrs. Dunstable closed the blade and flicked it open again, closed and flicked it open.

"You killed her?" I whispered.

"Oh yes. Well I had to, didn't I? She wouldn't tell me where she'd hidden my baby. Then she said she was going to tell on Matthew about the drugs, for his own good. I know what those prisons are like, I read the newspapers. A mother has a right to protect her children, doesn't she?"

I wanted to keep her talking to stall for time. "So you took the journal?"

"I had to kill her first. It was so easy," she said, wonder in her voice. "I met her by the river so Ian wouldn't know. I brought some tea in a thermos and gave her some. I listened to her tell her lies, waited for her to fall asleep. It didn't take long. I had these pills at home, you see, from before, when I was sick. I left the bottle in the car."

"How did you get her to take her clothes off?"

Mrs. Dunstable shook her head. "I didn't like that part, don't think I did. I'm not that kind! But her clothes: even her underwear was silk, lovely material. I had a terrible time getting them off without ripping anything."

"You left her shoes on."

"Disgusting shoes," she sneered. She took a step forward, swaying on her new heels. "No one should wear shoes that colour, Satan's colour. But I never thought they'd stay on." She giggled. "Must have given you quite a turn when you saw them. Red shoes on a naked corpse. I laughed, I did, when I read it in the paper."

"It wasn't funny."

"Depends on how you look at it." She stifled another fit of laughter. All the time, she kept flicking the knife blade in and out.

"You kept her briefcase," I said, urging her to continue.

"Of course, I had to find out where she'd hidden my baby. But she only had one file in it, in some kind of code." She patted the purse. "She had a diary too, the kind that locks. I wasn't going to read it," she shook her head. "I know better than to interfere with other people's private matters. But I had to know. I had a right to know. It broke my heart to scratch up that fine leather."

"That's where you found out about Matty and Gary Donnelly."

"Don't mention that man's name to me," she shouted. "If Matthew had never met him, he'd be here now, he'd be helping me."

"What about Mr. Dunstable? Did you tell him about Jennifer?"

She laughed that horrible croaking wheeze again. "Do you think I'm crazy?" she spluttered. "Ian's so hopeless. After you found Rumble, he went to Toronto to talk to Whitman. He said someone else in town had given them money for the same baby. All he was worried about was the money, about what the brethren would do when they found out it was all gone."

"Why didn't he go to the police?"

"Harper and Whitman threatened they'd turn Matthew in for drug dealing. Ian was mortified. He prayed all night. As if that would do any good. He wouldn't talk to me, of course. I was no use, he said, it was all my fault that Matthew turned bad, all my fault that we used church money to get my baby. He was worried that Rumble may have threatened the boy and he did something to her."

"Why didn't you tell him it was you?"

"I'm not stupid," she snarled.

"Sorry." I was desperate for her to continue. If she was planning to leave soon, she may already have ordered a cab. The driver could be here any minute. "What happened then?"

"Harper came here looking for the file and the diary. Ian first thought you had them and then that Matthew did. So I gave them to him. Oh yes, I did." She stroked the translucent plastic handle.

"Gary's truck was seen at the chapel," I said. "But the police think your husband killed himself because of Matthew."

"Ian wanted to turn Matthew in, because of the drugs. I persuaded him to think about it first. I said, Go to the chapel and pray. God will show you the way, I said. Then I phoned Mr. Donnelly and told him he had to drive me out there and wait for me. Well, I don't know how to drive, do I? Ian would never let me learn. He said I didn't need to know."

"I don't believe this," I muttered, shaking my head.

She heard me and smiled. "It's all true," her voice was as calm as if she was giving me cookie recipes. "I went up to Ian's office. I told him I couldn't talk in the church, that I wanted to sit in the car. I said I had a confession. He didn't want to listen, but he finally agreed. I had Matty's school thermos with me filled with coffee. Ian loved my coffee. I'd saved some of the pills from before, just in case. They worked so well the first time." She looked vaguely around the room. "Then I got out and attached the hose the way I'd seen it done on TV. Stuffed the crack in the window with his own scarf, and left the motor running."

"The police say it was suicide."

"I told them Ian had been troubled lately. And then they found out about the missing money." She stared at me, her teeth worrying at her lips. "Am I boring you, dear?" she asked.

"No, not at all," I said. How silly my words sounded. I couldn't keep my eyes off the knife.

"I said my prescription was missing, and that I'd thought Ian had taken it to help him sleep. They believed me. Why not? The coroner told me he must have taken them all at once so that he couldn't change his mind about dying." She snickered. "He was right about that part of it anyway."

"Why did you leave the folder with him?"

"In case they were suspicious. The folder shows Ian knew

Rumble and perhaps she was the one who got him to steal the money. Which is true, in a way. He killed Miss Rumble and then couldn't live with the guilt. It could have happened that way."

"And Gary?"

"He waited out front, just like I told him to. I hoped someone would see the truck and remember. Then, if there were any suspicions about Ian's death, he would get the blame. If he said he took me there, I'd deny it. Who would the police believe, a drug addict ex-con or me, the grieving widow?"

"You had it all thought out."

"I'm glad you think so. I plan pretty well if I do say so myself. Except for Matthew leaving. He shouldn't have left me alone like that."

"And now?"

"I'm leaving for Saskatchewan." She looked at her watch. "The airport taxi will be here any minute. But first, I have to take care of you."

I fell sideways off the chair as she rushed at the table, the knife descending in a glittering streak. It squealed across the formica top. I scrambled through the legs to the other side. She stared at me, her chest heaving. Some of the hair had escaped her bun; she tucked it behind her ear and smiled with a dreadful stretching of her painted lips.

"It's no use," she wheedled. "You can't get out, I've locked the door and you can't open it without a key. This will only take a minute. I'll be fast, it won't hurt. I used to look after the chickens on my daddy's farm, I know about clean kills."

I looked around for any weapon. Nothing. She began to circle the table and I did the same, my hands on the metal rim, keeping as much space as possible between us. I bumped into one of the chairs and it crashed to the ground. I didn't take my eyes off hers.

"Why are you going to Saskatchewan?" I asked. "Is that where you're from?"

"No, no, that's where my baby is. Rumble had the address in her little book. I'm just going to get my baby girl. That suitcase is full of clothes for her."

"You can't mean it? You wouldn't kidnap her?"

"They took her from me. She belongs to me." Mrs. Dunstable began to move faster. My hand touched the other chair back. I stopped and pulled it away from the table, its feet squeaking across the floor.

"Whitman told me the baby was placed there two years ago. She's three years old now. None of those clothes will fit."

"You believed him? They're all liars, all of them." She lunged at me again.

I heaved the chair at her. She screamed. The knife flew across the kitchen, thudded to the floor by the open door of the refrigerator and slid underneath. We both dived for it.

She was on top of me, her knees gouging into my thighs, one hand grappling my wrist, the other squeezing my throat. I grabbed her hair and yanked as hard as I could while my right hand clawed her wrist. She let go of my neck, her fingers scraping down my cheek as she aimed for my eyes. I bit her hand, all the time twisting and wriggling to get out from under her. She pummelled my breasts; one bony knee dug into my stomach. I heaved her off at last, scrambled up, and ran to the kitchen door. It was locked. I began to edge around the room towards the only other entrance.

Mrs. Dunstable, on her feet again, shoved the fridge; it teetered and crashed. She grabbed the knife. Smiling, she turned to confront me, her hair in long snakes about her face.

"Mother, what are you doing?"

The back door swung open. Matty stood there, key in his hand. Behind him was Gary Donnelly.

"Watch out, Matty," I cried. "She's got your knife."

Matty stepped into the room. "Mom?" His voice was small. "Mom, give me the knife."

She stood backed up against the wall, her new dress torn at one shoulder. She'd lost her shoes in the fight, but held the knife blade steady.

"Go away," she said in a harsh whisper. "This has nothing to do with you."

"I told you," Gary said. "Your old lady's nuts. She was with your Dad at the back of the church for a long time, Matty. She must have said something or done something to him."

"Is that true?" Matty stopped at the kitchen table. He wore khaki pants; a long-sleeved cotton shirt hid the tattoo I remembered seeing on his left arm. His hair was much longer and combed straight back from his forehead, a smooth pelt. The earring was a discrete gold ring.

"He was going to cause trouble," she said impatiently. "I told you to leave for your own good. Go now." She gestured at me with the knife. "I can take care of this too."

"Did you kill Dad?" Matty's voice broke.

She looked at him for the first time, surprised. "He was going to turn you in, Matthew. I had to."

"Damn you." The boy rushed his mother.

"No," she screamed as he butted his head into her belly and she fell, her arms wrapping around him, pulling him down with her. Gary was there instantly, prying them apart. She held on fiercely, but the two men were too much for her. She let go. The knife had been kicked aside in the fight. I edged around the three of them, creeping towards the door. They were past noticing me. Mrs. Dunstable curled on the floor, arms over her head, weeping. Matty stood over her, his head lowered, his fists balled at his side.

Gary, one hand on the boy's shoulder, soothed him. "Take it easy. She's still your mother. She needs help, we'll get her some help."

Then I was outside, alive and free.

An old man sat on the stoop of the house next door, a cigarette between his teeth. In one hand, he held a thin rope; at its end, a sleek black cat hunted bugs in a newly dug garden. I leaned heavily against the fence.

"Please," I said. "Call the police. Right now."

He took the butt from his mouth, looked at it, then looked me up and down. "Trouble?" he asked.

"Yes." I was impatient. Three of the buttons of my shirt had been pulled off in the struggle. I held it closed.

"The boy's back again. Is that it?" The old man began to reel in the cat, winding the cord around his fist. The beast fought the leash every step of the way. "Come on now, Pretty," the man said. "Be a good girl for Daddy."

"Who's she?" An immensely fat woman appeared at the door. She squinted against the sun's glare.

The man picked up his cat and stood up slowly, groaning slightly. He bent over suddenly in a fit of coughing, spat, and straightened. He nodded at the Dunstable house.

"We don't want no more trouble from them," he said. He slammed the screen door shut and faded away into the shadows inside.

I pushed away from the fence and opened the back gate. Gary's truck was parked in the alley.

"Mrs. Cairns, Mrs. Cairns," Matty called.

I ran.

SEVENTEEN

Right now, I am sitting on the top step of my verandah. I finger my key ring, heavy now with all the locks I own: the car; this house, front door and back; the high-rise lobby; the door to the bachelorette. A U-Haul van is parked at the curb. We finished loading it last night with the furniture I'll need, the boxes of books, clothes, and dishes. Will is going to drive me down to the city to help me settle into my little apartment. He has already given me a housewarming gift, an etching by a local artist of the river reeds at sunset.

Karen sits on the grass, her bicycle beside her. She has come to say good-bye. She'll stay with Sadie until Will gets back later next week. We've been drinking champagne and the dark green glass of the bottle absorbs and glows with light as she lifts it to her mouth. I'll miss Karen.

I can see the gates of the park although the trees, heavy with leaves, bend low over the sidewalk, almost obscuring the view of the river. The water sparkles in the sun, the fall over the dam a cheerful murmur. Crickets are singing in the tall grass of the football field and a killdeer flies up, frantic, circling before it disappears in the railway ditch. I can see Will now and Sadie. He throws a stick for her and she leaps, catching it in mid-air. She runs back to him, but when he tries to take the stick from her, she shakes her head. I know she is growling, teasing him into her favourite game. He looks up, catches sight of me, and waves. I finger the keys, loose in my hand.

"So it's really all over now?" Karen asks. She passes me the bottle and lies back, a blade of grass between her teeth.

"I think so. Hope so, anyway. Matty's in a treatment centre for drugs, did you know?"

"Cindy told me. She visited Gary in prison."

"Is she going to go back to him?"

"No. But she wanted him to know about the baby and the Lorings. She told me that he feels pretty guilty about running out on her. He still might turn out all right. He did persuade Matty to come back, after all, and kept Mrs. Dunstable from killing you. I never would have guessed her capable of murder."

A cloud obscures the sun for a moment. Will looks up from his game to scan the sky. He clips Sadie's leash to her collar. I stand up and he waves again. I watch the two of them as they come through the gates.

"Time to go."

Karen upends the bottle into the grass and walks with me to the curb.

I stroke the warm flank of the van. "Hard to believe I'm really going," I say.

"Are you sure you know what you're doing?" She blushes at the look I give her. "I know, I know, we've been through this a hundred times. But it's still not too late to change your mind. You could commute from here."

"Every day? You must be joking. It might seem crazy, but it's the right thing to do. For both of us."

Sadie is with us now, licking our hands. Will hands Karen the leash. "Ready?" he says to me.

I look at the house, slipping the keys into my coat pocket. Will walks around the van, tests the rear door handle one more time, then climbs in behind the wheel. The motor sputters and roars.

"Come and visit real soon," I hug Karen, hard.

After a moment, she hugs back. "You won't be going to

classes all the time," she says. "What are you going to do with yourself?

I kneel by Sadie, ruffling her ears. She closes her eyes, her lips open in a wide doggy smile, tongue lolling. I smile up at my friend.

"I don't know," I say. "But something different."